"I'm a private person."

"You used to be, but not anymore. Not since your book hit the bestseller lists and stayed there."

"Drip, drip, drip," he said.

"What does that mean?"

"You're like water on a rock, wearing it down."

She lifted her chin. "I like to think that's one of my best qualities."

"It's good." Jack's gaze dropped to her chest, and the glitter was back in his eyes. "But not your best."

He didn't miss much, so she was pretty sure he could tell that the pulse in her neck had just gone from normal to racing. There was only one way to interpret those words and that look. He moved closer and she held her breath, hoping that he was going to kiss her. Heat from his body warmed her skin when he stopped right in front of her.

* * *

THE BACHELORS OF BLACKWATER LAKE:
They won't be single for long!

Dear Reader,

Writing is a solitary profession, and finding the balance between work and play can sometimes be a challenge. Authors tend to lose themselves in a story and characters, and the catch-22 is getting out of that made-up world to the real one—where one experiences life, observes people and fills up the creative well. And when one doesn't live alone, carving out the kind of space necessary for your imagination to run wild turns into a delicate dance. It requires both tact and toughness.

In *A Word with the Bachelor*, bestselling author Jack Garner has the toughness down to a T. It's the tact part he needs to work on when book coach Erin Riley arrives on his isolated Blackwater Lake doorstep to jumpstart his Muse. Book number two is late, and the pretty, perky English teacher's presence is the price he has to pay for a deadline extension. But he figures, like every other woman in his life, she'll leave when the going gets rocky.

The only problem is Jack underestimates Erin's determination to get the job done. She is the opposite of a pushover and her sunny disposition camouflages the steely resolve that sustained her through the loss of someone important to her. The ex-military lone wolf is not happy about sharing his space, and even more crabby when she tempts him to share his heart. And so the battle of wills is on!

The only thing more fun than writing books is creating a character who writes books. This story is close to my own heart and I hope you enjoy it.

Happy Reading!

Teresa Southwick

A Word with the Bachelor

Teresa Southwick

HARLEQUIN® SPECIAL EDITION®

Recycling programs
for this product may
not exist in your area.

ISBN-13: 978-0-373-65982-1

A Word with the Bachelor

Copyright © 2016 by Teresa Southwick

All rights reserved. Except for use in any review, the reproduction or utilization of this work in whole or in part in any form by any electronic, mechanical or other means, now known or hereinafter invented, including xerography, photocopying and recording, or in any information storage or retrieval system, is forbidden without the written permission of the publisher, Harlequin Enterprises Limited, 225 Duncan Mill Road, Don Mills, Ontario M3B 3K9, Canada.

This is a work of fiction. Names, characters, places and incidents are either the product of the author's imagination or are used fictitiously, and any resemblance to actual persons, living or dead, business establishments, events or locales is entirely coincidental.

This edition published by arrangement with Harlequin Books S.A.

For questions and comments about the quality of this book, please contact us at CustomerService@Harlequin.com.

® and TM are trademarks of Harlequin Enterprises Limited or its corporate affiliates. Trademarks indicated with ® are registered in the United States Patent and Trademark Office, the Canadian Intellectual Property Office and in other countries.

Printed in U.S.A.

www.Harlequin.com

Teresa Southwick lives with her husband in Las Vegas, the city that reinvents itself every day. An avid fan of romance novels, she is delighted to be living out her dream of writing for Harlequin.

Visit the Author Profile page at Harlequin.com for more titles.

To educators Andrea Verga Pascale and her husband, John Pascale. The influence of a good teacher can never be erased and you guys are the best! When I sit down to write, I'm so grateful to my former teachers for giving me the necessary tools to do what I love. Never doubt that every student you meet is all the better for having had you in their life. You touch the world. You teach!

Chapter One

She'd been warned that Jack Garner would be difficult but no one had prepared her for his overwhelming sex appeal.

If Erin Riley had known the author was more buff and better-looking than the guy on the cover of his action-adventure novel, she wasn't sure she'd have taken this job as his book coach. Quite possibly she was in over her head. She'd already failed the first test by not researching the man she would be working for. He'd just answered her knock on his door and all she could do was stare.

"Are you selling something?" He glanced at her wheeled suitcase.

"No. Sorry." She took a deep, cleansing breath. "I'm Erin Riley. Cheryl Kavanagh sent me."

"My editor." His dark blue eyes narrowed. "Cut the crap."

"Excuse me?"

"You're here to babysit me." He glanced over his shoulder and called, "Harley!"

Moments later some black-and-white creature ran outside, stopped beside Jack and looked up adoringly. Erin could respect the feeling.

Jack closed the front door and proceeded down the three steps. "Walk."

She wasn't sure if he meant her, but left the suitcase on the porch and hurried after him. That's when she realized the creature was without a doubt the ugliest dog she'd ever seen. It looked like a four-legged elf, a mythical being straight out of *The Hobbit*. The thing was small with a hairy head that didn't look substantial enough to hold up the ginormous ears. Stick legs had tufts of fur by the paws and some kind of garment made of camouflage material covered the skinny, hairless body.

Fascination with the dog would have to wait. She moved quickly to catch up to the man. For him and his long legs it might be considered a walk, but she nearly had to jog to keep up. He was headed toward Blackwater Lake—the body of water from which this small town in Montana took its name.

"Mr. Garner—"

"Jack."

She assumed that meant he was giving her permission to call him by his first name. "All right. Jack."

They passed a building on the dock that said Blackwater Lake Marina and Bait Shop. Almost all of the slips in the natural bay were full, and held small boats and some that looked more luxurious and big enough to sleep on.

The scenery was nearly as breathtaking as trying to keep up with Jack. Dark blue lake water stretched ahead of her as far as the eye could see and bumped up against some impressive mountains. Overhead, the blue of the sky was only interrupted by wispy white clouds. It was quiet and serene, a place that on the surface looked to be a perfect writing environment. But if that was the case, she wouldn't be here.

"So, Jack—"

"Harley, stand down."

The small dog stopped chasing and barking at the little brown birds that had been pecking in the sketchy grass beside the lake. They took off and the homely animal instantly moved into step beside his human as ordered.

"Girl or boy?" she asked.

"What?" Jack gave her a wary sideways look.

"Is the dog male or female?"

"Male."

"That's unexpected."

"Meaning?"

"I would never have figured a guy like you to have a dog like this."

"Are you insulting my dog?"

Oh, boy. How did she put into words that she'd been profiling and figured a manly man like Jack Garner would have a big, burly guy dog. Pit bull. Rottweiler. Bulldog. The problem was the ugly little animal didn't seem compatible with a man who'd spent a good number of years in the United States Army Special Forces Operations, Ranger Battalion. She only knew that from reading his book and the short bio in the back.

Finding the words was like trying to navigate a minefield. "I just… The two of you are—" She sighed.

"What's wrong with him?"

"Nothing." Aside from not being very attractive. Unlike his owner, who was so attractive her toes were curling. There were a lot of things she could say. *Beauty is in the eye of the beholder. Beauty is only skin deep. Don't judge a book by its cover.* She finally settled on a question. "Why did you pick him?"

"It's classified."

He could tell her, but he'd have to kill her? He looked like he wanted to do that anyway.

"Okay," she said. "What kind of dog is he?"

"A Chinese crested."

"I see. Sounds noble." She knew very little about dogs.

"Don't judge a book by its cover."

Did she get points for not saying that? At least it was the segue she'd been waiting for. "Speaking of books—"

"Cheryl wants to know where mine is." Anger and frustration were wrapped around the words.

"Look at it from her perspective. Your first book is incredibly successful. Even more amazing because there was no promotion." He'd refused to do any. "Word-of-mouth has been unbelievably effective. And it's been optioned for a movie. That's an impressive springboard for a second book."

"The manuscript is a little late," he conceded.

"Nine months late. You could make a baby in that length of time." Did she really just say that out loud? "Not judging," she added.

The look he shot her was as black as his hair. In worn jeans and a faded olive-green T-shirt, his toned and muscular body was displayed to perfection. She'd read that it was instinctive for a woman to mate with a strong male who could protect her and any offspring she produced. Right this second her female instincts were going nuts.

"Meaning what?" His voice was low, just north of irritated, and creeping into superannoyed territory.

It was an alpha-male tone meant to intimidate, but if Erin let him get to her now, this book-coach thing was never going to work and she really wanted it to. She wanted to help. To do that, she had to stand up to him right now.

"Don't play games, Jack. You know why I'm here.

You're late on your deadline and refuse to take your editor's calls. Or your agent's, for that matter. Everyone wants to build on the momentum of your phenomenally successful first book. Cheryl said you have the most raw talent of any writer she's seen in a very long time. So, she sent me here to help you focus."

"Why?"

"You know the answer to that question, but I'll spell it out anyway. There's a lot of money at stake. Millions," she said. "Your editor is in your corner. She'll do whatever she can."

"No, I meant why you?"

He was asking for a resumé so she'd give him a verbal one. Harley walked over and started sniffing her so Erin stopped and bent to scratch his head. "My cousin is an editorial assistant at the publishing house and recommended me."

"Why?"

"I have a master's degree in English and literature. And I've taught high-school honors English, AP classes and community-college writing courses."

"Why aren't you in school now? It's after Labor Day."

"I'm a substitute. That means I can tell them when I'm available." The arrangement had worked when her fiancé, Garrett, was terminally ill. The money was good and after his death a year and a half ago she hadn't changed her status to full-time. "Do you know Corinne Carlisle?"

"No."

"She's one of Cheryl's authors, a cozy mystery writer. This summer she was having trouble finishing her manuscript. Through my cousin I was hired to—"

"Babysit."

"Focus her." Erin had really enjoyed the job and wanted to do more. She and Garrett had talked about traveling the world, but he got sick and they never had the chance. Assignments like this let her go places she might not otherwise see and, if asked, she wanted to do more of this. "She was a delightful lady to work with."

Harley stood still at his feet and Jack picked him up. It was automatic, instinctive, as if that was their rhythm. "I'm not delightful."

"Harley might beg to differ."

Under Jack's big, gently stroking hand the unattractive animal looked to be in doggy heaven. Erin had the most erotic sensation, as if his hand was brushing over her bare skin. Shivers hopped, skipped and jumped down her spine.

"He'd be wrong."

"Look, I was able to help Corinne finish her book. I can do the same for you. I'm good at research. I can critique and edit and brainstorm story ideas. And Cheryl strongly suggested that I make sure you eat three times a day. Your home is ideal for this arrangement with the separate upstairs and downstairs apartments."

A good thing, too, because Blackwater Lake was small. There was a lodge close by, but it had been completely booked and there wouldn't be more in the way of accommodations until the resort under construction was completed.

The look on Jack's face showed a lot of regret and it was probably about the fact that he'd shared details of his duplex home with his editor. "My office is up. I live down."

Erin was very aware that he was trying to scare her off but the technique was useless on her. Jack didn't know that when you faced cancer with someone you cared about there wasn't a lot left to be afraid of. "I won't take up much room."

With Harley in his arms he started walking back the way they'd come. "I got a message from Cheryl."

"Oh?"

"If I want a deadline extension you're the price I have to pay for it."

"Great."

"Not." He stopped walking and stared at her.

"Okay, I get it. You don't want me here."

"If I could fire you I would," he confirmed.

"You could give back the advance."

The glare he shot her almost made his eyes glow. "Abandoning the mission isn't an option."

She studied the brooding man. The sight of the dozing, completely trusting ugly little dog in his arms was so at odds with the hostile, confrontational image he was projecting to her. Somewhere inside him was a guy who'd chosen and was good to a small, homely animal. That was a man she wanted to know. And then there was the powerful, startling, confusing and off-putting attraction she'd felt from the moment he'd answered his door.

"I'm here to be of service."

He stared at her and his mouth tightened. "We're not sleeping together if that's what you're thinking."

"I'm sorry— What?"

Holy smokes! Her cheeks burned and it had nothing to do with the sun shining down from that big, blue sky. How did he know? She hadn't exactly been thinking about sex, but close enough to be humiliated by what he'd said.

"I didn't— I never—"

"I need to know if you can do this job and not look at me like that."

"I'm not looking at you any way," she protested.

He shook his head. "Your face is so easy to read."

"No, it's not."

"And you're a bad liar." He looked closer. "Have you even been with a man?"

That question was getting awfully close to the one nerve

she had left and she figured it was a deliberate attempt to get on it.

"Yes, I've been with a man." She looked up and met his gaze. If she was really that easy to read he would see her defiance and determination. "I was engaged."

"That's need-to-know and I don't need to."

"Okay then. I guess we understand each other."

Jack didn't understand Little Miss Perky at all. In the less than twenty-four hours since her arrival he'd been nothing more than barely civil and yet she was still here. Like an eager puppy.

"So let's talk about the book," she said, putting a mug on his desk in front of him.

Jack looked at it and didn't miss the fact that there was now a coaster for his cup that covered the circular coffee stain he'd grown fond of. That was kind of like shutting the barn door after the horse got out.

He leaned back in his cushy leather chair, a splurge from the unexpectedly astounding royalties on his first book, and met her gaze. "Let's talk about my office instead."

"What about it?"

He could actually see the oak top of his desk, whereas before only that circular spot had been visible. Pens, pencils, Post-its, a highlighter, et cetera, were…annoyingly organized. His mug with the army insignia on it that was for display purposes only was conspicuously full of writing implements. Yesterday, before she'd shown up, there were yellow legal pads scattered on the ratty chair and thrift-shop tables in this room and now they were nowhere to be seen. He didn't know where anything was.

"Things aren't where I put them."

"I tidied up. I was awake early and didn't want to start

breakfast too early in case you liked to sleep in." She shrugged. "So I made myself useful."

"In what universe? A man's office is sacred ground." The up and down apartments on the property were identical floor plans with two bedrooms and bathrooms. In addition to the isolation out here by the lake he'd liked the idea of separate spaces for work and living. Now Erin Riley had invaded both. Last night she'd slept upstairs in the spare room with unfettered access to his office. That was going to change. "I like my stuff out so I can find it."

She sat in one of the chairs facing the desk, clearly not discouraged by his inhospitable reception and intending to dig in. "Understood."

Jack squirmed a little, unable to shake the sensation that he'd drop-kicked a kitten. She was trying to do her job and he wasn't making it easy. Because he didn't want her here poking into things. All he needed was time to work through his creative speed bumps.

"If you want to be useful," he said, "I need supplies. Like you said last night, there's not much food here to work with."

But she'd proved to be resourceful and managed to make dinner. With some eggs, a few vegetables and ground beef she'd whipped up a tasty skillet dish. This morning was grilled cheese sandwiches. When he'd reminded her it wasn't lunch yet, she'd said his stomach didn't know what time it was. As if he didn't already know that. Special Forces training highlighted the need for nourishment to keep the body in tip-top working order and sometimes that meant making do with what was available. He'd just been messing with her because that sandwich tasted pretty darn good.

The thing was, her perky disposition never slipped. Like yesterday when he'd said he wouldn't sleep with her, she'd calmly handled him. The only clue that he'd made her uncomfortable was the high color in her cheeks. Women weren't top secret to him; he knew when one liked what she saw. And from the moment he'd answered the door to Erin Riley, she'd looked at him that way. If she could see inside him, she'd run in the opposite direction.

Maybe this attitude of his was a way of initiating her, like boot camp, to see if he could get her to crack. If so, that made him a son of a bitch and he felt a little guilt, but managed to ignore it. Her insertion into his life hadn't been his idea. But like he'd said—he couldn't fire her. All he could do was discourage her.

So far that was a negative on dissuasion. Her sunny disposition made him want to put on his shades. Looking at her was like coming out of a pitch-dark room into light so bright it made your eyes hurt. Even her shoulder-length brown hair had sunlit, cheerful streaks running through it. And flecks of gold brightened her pretty green eyes. She wasn't extraordinarily beautiful, not like his ex-wife. But she was vulnerable, yet strong—a compelling combination somehow and he didn't want to be compelled.

"Jack?"

Hearing her say his name snapped him back. "What?"

"Talking about your work-in-progress might get the creative juices flowing."

"That's not my process," he said stubbornly.

"Okay." She thought for a moment. "Then let's talk about what your process is."

"You're like a pit bull." Harley was in his bed beside the desk and he reached down to scratch the dog's head. Instantly the animal rolled onto his back and Jack almost smiled. "Once you sink your teeth in you don't let go."

"Nice try." Those flecks in her eyes darkened, making them more brown than green. She looked like a teacher who'd just figured out someone was attempting to pull a fast one. "You're trying to deflect attention from yourself. Let's get something straight, Jack. This isn't about me."

So that flanking maneuver didn't work. Time for a contingency plan. "I have the situation under control."

"Good. All you have to do is give Cheryl a firm date for manuscript delivery."

He couldn't exactly do that. "I'm still working out some plot details."

"Okay. So let's talk about that."

"Look, Erin, my name and mine alone is on the front of the book. The content is my personal responsibility and I take that very seriously. I don't write by committee."

"Ah," she said, as if just understanding something.

"What does that mean?" He was pretty sure his facial expression wasn't easy to read, unlike hers.

"I had a similar conversation when I worked with Corinne Carlisle. She was uncomfortable in the beginning of our cooperative efforts. A clandestine collaboration, she called it. I thought that was a personal quirk of hers, or a chick thing."

"It wasn't?"

She shook her head. "I believe it's a writer thing."

"Call it what you want. I just prefer to work alone."

His gaze was drawn to her legs when she crossed one over the other. The jeans she was wearing were a little loose and left too much to the imagination because he suspected the hidden curves would be well worth a look. Probably a good thing the denim wasn't skintight. It would only be a distraction that he didn't want or need.

"Alone." She nodded her understanding of his statement. "I heard you were a loner."

"Oh?"

"Cheryl explained the downside of this assignment. She made sure I knew that you don't play well with others."

The words hung in the air between them for several moments. Jack couldn't tell whether or not that was a criticism. It really didn't matter. On the upside, maybe she was finally getting the message.

"By definition a loner needs to be alone."

"I understand." Her tone was soothing, like a shrink would use, or a hostage negotiator.

"Don't patronize me," he said.

"I'm sorry you feel I'm doing that. It wasn't my intention." She stopped for a moment, thinking, as if to come up with the right words to make him understand. "I respect your commitment to responsibility in writing the book you want to write. But I have undertaken this assignment and Cheryl is expecting tangible results. I'm not backing down from the challenge of you. It's best you accept that. So, we have to start somewhere."

"And you think talking about the story is the way to go."

"It worked for Corinne." She folded her hands in her lap. "If you have a better idea that would be awesome."

"Look, I appreciate your willingness and enthusiasm." Although he could think of better uses for it. "But I write action-adventure. A woman like you has no frame of reference for that so talking is a complete waste of time."

"I haven't been in the military or gone to war if that's what you're saying. But I read extensively and go to the movies. I can help you dissect the plot. I have ideas and that can be helpful."

He'd started his last book as a therapeutic exercise to work through all the crap life had thrown at him. Pulling that stuff up was like exposing his soul. Doing that with her just wasn't going to happen. For reasons he couldn't explain, he didn't want her to see the darkness inside him.

"Ideas?" He leaned forward and rested his forearms on the unnaturally tidy top of his desk. "You're Pollyanna. No offense, but you can't possibly have suggestions for what I write."

"Really?" She sat up straighter in the chair, almost literally stiffening her spine.

"In my opinion, yes."

"It's hard to form an opinion without information and you don't know anything about me if you truly believe I've had no life experiences."

"So you were engaged. There was a proposal. Probably a ring. Not a big deal." He saw something slip into her eyes but it didn't stop him. He'd been engaged once, too, even took the next step and got married. It didn't work out for a lot of reasons, but mostly he wasn't very good at being a husband. "Since you used past tense I guess you broke up with him. Still not gritty—"

"He died. Whether it happens in a war zone or the home front, death is not pretty. It's raw and painful. I think that qualifies as life experience."

He studied her and realized his mission, real or invented, had been successful. He'd managed to put clouds in her eyes and make the sunshine disappear.

Damned if he didn't want to undo what he'd just done.

Chapter Two

Erin sat in the passenger seat of Jack's rugged jeep trying to figure him out. First he'd said he had no use for her, then later in the afternoon offered to take her into town. She had a long-term rental car from the airport and was prepared to shop on her own, but he'd insisted on driving. His excuse was that they might as well buy supplies together, but she had a sneaking suspicion there was another reason. One that would tarnish his tough-guy image.

"So, Jack," she began, "I think your ogre act is just that. An act."

He turned right onto Lakeview Drive, then gave her a quick, questioning look. "I have no idea what you're talking about."

"You were all gruff and abrupt earlier. Patronizing me about a ring, a proposal and a broken engagement being the equivalent of a hangnail in the action-adventure world."

"It is." His profile could have been carved in stone on Mt. Rushmore. It was all sharp angles and hard lines.

"But when I corrected your assumption that I was shallow and typical by revealing that I lost someone close to me, I think you felt bad about jumping to conclusions and invited me to go shopping to make up for it."

There was another glance in her direction before he returned his gaze to the road. "In the army I operated on gut instinct and never second-guessed my actions."

"That was training for combat situations. In the regular world you replay a conversation and sometimes regret responses. It's normal. You asked me to go shopping because you can't take back what you said and are trying to be nice."

"Are you serious?"

"Completely." She adjusted her sunglasses. It was a beautiful day in late September and this road to town went around the lake. The surface of the water sparkled like diamonds as the sun sank lower in the cloudless blue sky. "The problem is that your nice muscles haven't been stretched in a while."

"You know what I think?"

"Not a clue," she said, wishing she could see his eyes behind those too-sexy-for-words aviator sunglasses. "But I bet you're going to tell me."

"Damn straight." He looked over, his mouth pulled into a straight line. "I think you're a fugitive from fantasyland."

That would be a step up for her after nursing Garrett through cancer and watching him take his last breath. "Oh?"

"I'm not a nice man. If you were smart, you'd ditch this job and get the hell out of here. Away from me."

"Hmm."

"What does that mean?"

"You think I'm fragile and I think you're a fraud. So what we have here is a standoff."

"Guess so," he said. "Sooner or later one of us is going to blink and it won't be me."

"Sounds like a challenge or a treaty to me. Maybe both." It was going to take a lot of convincing to make her believe he was as unfeeling as he wanted her to think he was.

"For the record, it makes good sense to coordinate shopping since you'll be doing the cooking and don't know what Harley likes."

That made her smile. Big bad warrior was hiding behind the world's most unattractive dog. But she just said, "Understood."

"You hungry?" The words were unexpected, but they were nearing the Blackwater Lake city limits.

"Starving."

"Me, too. Let's get something to eat." He glanced over quickly as if checking to see whether or not she'd noticed him being nice. "Grocery shopping will go easier that way."

"I think so, too." And that's the first time they'd agreed on anything in the last twenty-four hours.

He stopped the jeep at a stand-alone building near the end of Main Street, not far from city hall. There was a sign on the outside that read Bar None, with crossed cocktail glasses on it.

"Don't tell me," she said. "I'm driving you to drink."

"You said it, not me." But his teeth flashed in a fleeting smile before he got out of the car.

Erin opened her door and slid to the ground, then met him on the sidewalk. The wooden exterior was reminiscent of a miner's shack and the heavy oak door had a vertical brass handle. Jack grabbed it and pulled the door open for her.

The pulse in her neck jumped as she passed him and walked inside. Heat from his body was enough to sizzle her senses and short them out. That was probably the reason it seemed to take longer than usual for her eyes to grow accustomed to the dim interior after being outside.

"This looks nice," she finally said.

"It's okay."

Lining the walls were booths with leather seats and lantern-shaped lights. Dark beams ran the length of the ceiling and old wooden planks covered the floor. An oak bar with a brass footrail commanded the center of the room.

"Table or booth?"

She scanned the bistro tables scattered over the floor. "Where do you usually sit?"

"At the bar."

She should have guessed and would have if she wasn't standing so close to Jack. Worn jeans, gray hoodie over tight black T-shirt, scuffed boots. This was as much a uniform for him as the camouflage he'd no doubt worn in the military. He'd been so right about what she was thinking yesterday. Not so much about sleeping with him, although she'd gotten as far as wondering what he looked like naked. But she found him incredibly hot and was mortified that he'd been able to see that.

Now she needed to conceal the fact that her instantaneous attraction had not yet run its course, or she'd be risking losing this job.

"The bar it is." She followed him across the room.

It was closing in on five o'clock and there were only a handful of people in the place. Jack headed for the bar and took a seat on one of the stools beside a tall, broad-shouldered, handsome man in a khaki uniform.

"Hey, Sheriff," he said. "I see you changed your mind about leaving town."

The man smiled and held out his hand. "Good to see you. Been a while, Jack. If you came around more, you'd know that my dad retired and I'm now the head lawman in town."

"I've been busy."

Erin managed to haul herself up on the stool next to him. Her legs were short; the chairs were high. It wasn't graceful. Jack looked at her then at the sheriff, but said nothing.

"Hi," the man said to her. "Haven't seen you around before."

She reached an arm in front of Jack and shook the sheriff's hand. "Erin Riley."

"Will Fletcher," he said.

A beautiful blue-eyed redhead walked over to them and stopped on the other side of the bar. "If it isn't Blackwater Lake's famous author."

"Hi, Delanie."

The woman looked from Jack to Erin and waited expectantly. Apparently she got tired of waiting because she asked, "Who's your friend?"

"Erin Riley." He rested his forearms on the bar. "And we're not friends."

"Nice to meet you, Erin." Delanie stared at Jack. "So, if you're not friends, what are you?"

The silence grew as all of them stared at Jack, waiting for clarification. He finally shrugged and said, "That's a good question."

Erin jumped in. "I'm his research assistant."

"Okay, then. What can I get you two?" Delanie asked. "Food? Drinks?"

"I'd like to see a menu, please. And a glass of chardonnay would be lovely."

"You got it." The woman grabbed two plastic-covered sheets containing the food choices and set them in front of her and Jack. Then she opened a bottle of white wine and poured a glass, putting it on a napkin in front of Erin. "Beer, Jack?"

"The usual."

"How long have you been in town?" Sheriff Fletcher asked.

"A day. So far I haven't seen much except the lake and marina. And Main Street. But Blackwater Lake is the most beautiful place I've ever been."

"Where are you from?" Delanie used a rag to wipe non-existent spots from the bar.

"Phoenix." The bar owner and the sheriff were nodding as if that explained a lot. "Don't judge. There's a beauty in the Arizona desert, too, it's just different. I actually haven't done much traveling, though, but I've always wanted to."

"So, you're a research assistant?" Sitting at the bar, the sheriff leaned his forearms on the edge of the oak. "Is that a permanent arrangement?"

Erin looked at Jack and he didn't seem inclined to answer so she was forced to wing it. "Not permanent. Just for the book in progress. I freelance and in between assignments I work as a substitute high school English teacher."

"So you're overqualified to read that menu," Jack said.

She got his point. He was hungry and wanted to get this over with. After scanning the list of options she said, "I'd like a club sandwich and side salad."

Jack never even looked at the choices. "Burger and fries."

"Coming right up," Delanie said, then disappeared in the back.

The sheriff stood and dropped some bills on the bar. "Good to see you, Jack. Don't be a stranger. Welcome, Erin. I hope you enjoy your stay here in Blackwater Lake. It is a pretty place. Take it from me. I left for a lot of years, but couldn't stay away. There are good people here."

"I look forward to meeting them."

"What's your hurry, Sheriff?" Jack hadn't been particularly social so the question was unexpected.

"I have paperwork to finish up at the office. Then I'm taking April out to dinner."

"Is that your wife?" Erin asked.

"Fiancée." Will Fletcher's rugged features softened when he smiled. "But us getting married is long overdue. We're making plans to rectify that. Can't be soon enough for me."

"Congratulations," she said.

"Thanks. Good luck with the book, Jack."

Erin had a feeling she was the one who needed luck *helping* Jack with the manuscript. His cooperation would be a good place to start. "He seems nice."

"I suppose."

"He said people are friendly. Have you met a lot of folks since you've been here?"

"No."

"Have you made an effort?"

"No."

"I'm going out on a limb here and say that everyone you've become acquainted with has been a customer here at Bar None."

There was a challenge in his eyes when he met her gaze. "So?"

"Have you ever heard the saying that 'no man is an island'? You have to reach out and meet people halfway. On top of that, writing doesn't happen in a vacuum. You have to fill up the creative well. That happens with experiences and to have those, being sociable helps."

"I'll keep that in mind."

"Good," she said.

"And, Erin?"

"Yes?"

"It occurs to me that the armed forces of the United States don't need to stockpile weapons. All the brass needs to do is turn you loose on the enemy to talk them to death."

She wondered whether or not to be offended by that, then decided one of them needed to be an optimist. "I'll take that as a compliment."

The morning after taking her to town, Jack went upstairs to his office, leaving Erin in the kitchen, cleaning up after breakfast. She was a good cook. If his editor ever spoke to him again he'd have to thank her for that. The omelet, fruit, toast and coffee was the best morning meal he'd had in a long time. Whatever he threw together was maybe one step above the army's MREs—meals ready to eat.

He turned on his laptop and opened the file "Mac Daniels," which was the name of his ex-army ranger, Special Forces hero. After reading through the pages he'd written, he said, "This sucks."

If the pages had been printed out, he'd have wadded them up and tossed the balls of paper across the room. They weren't and he deleted them. Right now he'd take a black ops mission over this. But army rangers never quit and he was literally on borrowed time with this project. After he'd left the military and his wife left him, he'd been pretty sure that being a soldier was the only thing he was good at.

Then he wrote a bestselling novel and the publisher wanted the second book on the two-book contract he'd signed, but he was late turning it in. What if he was a one-hit wonder? Maybe he *was* only good at soldiering. If he had to throw in the towel on this book, that would prove he'd been right.

The sheriff's words from yesterday drifted through his mind.

"Work in progress, my ass," he mumbled. He didn't need luck as much as inspiration.

There was a knock on the door and since he used the living room of the upstairs apartment for his office, technically the knock was on the office door. If he said nothing, would she go away?

Erin opened it and poked her head in. "Reporting for duty, sir."

Nine on the dot. It was as if she was punching a time clock. Harley ran inside and settled in his bed next to the desk. Little traitor had been hanging out with her.

Instead of inspiration, what he got was another challenge. "I work alone."

"Not any more" was what he expected out of her but that's not what she said.

"Let's talk about the book." She moved in front of the desk.

It was exactly what she'd said yesterday. "I'm a writer, not a talker."

A look crossed her face that said she'd noticed. "Tell me about the story. This is the sequel to *High Value Target*, so the hero is Mac Daniels."

He nodded an answer, if only to prove that he was telling the truth about the writer-versus-talker thing.

She tilted her head and shiny, gold-streaked brown hair slid over her shoulder. "I'm curious. When you named this character, did you mean for it to rhyme with Jack Daniel's, the whiskey? An inside joke? Or was it coincidence?"

Sharp girl, he thought. But the only answer he gave her was a small smile.

"Okay then. Moving on." She settled a hip on the corner of the desk and met his gaze. "I read the first book. Mac was a reluctant hero and took down the bad guys. What is his goal in this book?"

Jack wanted to squirm and this is where Ranger training came in handy, other than a war zone, of course. He'd learned how to stay in one position without moving for hours. "Mac is trying to stay alive."

"It's a good goal." She thought for a moment. "So who or what is standing in his way?"

"You mean who's after him?"

"*Is* someone after him? If so, why?"

Jack was still working out those details. It was what he did. On his own. This was *his* work-in-progress. His office. And that reminded him. "Look, Erin, there's something I'd like to talk to you about."

"Okay. That's what I'm here for."

"I'm not comfortable with this arrangement."

"And I'm not leaving." Her eyes flashed and her expression was locked and loaded on stubborn.

"No. I meant you bunking down up here." With unfettered access to his office. On top of that, the whole place was now filled with the scent of sunlight and flowers. And…her. How was he supposed to concentrate when his work space smelled like a girl?

"If you'd like I can pitch a tent outside," she said with more than a little sarcasm.

Jack wondered if that look on her face frightened the teenage boys in her English classes. It sure didn't work on him. For over ten years his job had been about dealing with life-and-death conflicts. Erin Riley didn't intimidate him at all.

"That won't be necessary." Although the idea was interesting, she didn't look like an outdoors kind of woman. More a hotel-and-happy-hour type. When she'd shown up and made it clear she wasn't leaving, he'd figured the spare room up here would be best. It wasn't. "I'd like to move you into the spare room downstairs."

"I don't want to throw your routine off—"

"Too late." He leaned back in his chair. "The thing is, if I want to work during the night, I wouldn't want to wake you."

"Whatever you want."

Jack happened to be looking at her mouth when she said that and the words turned into something that was a very bad idea. "Okay, then. Your job is to move your things to the spare bedroom downstairs."

"And afterward?"

"Isn't that enough?"

"I don't have much. That won't take very long. I'm here to assist. Tell me how to do that."

Yesterday at Bar None she'd introduced herself as his research assistant. That gave him an idea. "You know, it would help if you looked some things up for me."

"Great." That put the splashes of gold back in her green eyes. "What?"

"Why don't you go ahead and pack your stuff up and take it downstairs. I'll have a list ready when you're finished."

"Okay."

Erin disappeared down the hall but unfortunately the scent of her skin lingered in his work space. Later he would figure out how to man this place up again, but right now he had to do something to keep her busy and out of his hair.

Jack searched *gold* and *diamonds* on Google, figuring either one could put Mac Daniels's life on the line. As he browsed, something caught his eye. *Diamonds are a girl's best friend. Say it with diamonds.*

Erin came back into his office with her rolling suitcase and a bag she held in her hand. He had a sneaking suspicion that whatever made her smell so good was in the little one.

"I've got everything," she said cheerfully.

"That didn't take long."

"Told you it wouldn't." She headed for the door.

"Do you need help with those bags?"

"No. You keep working. I'll be back shortly to help."

Jack waited for the door to close and noted that Harley stayed where he was in his bed. "Good move, buddy. Never bite the hand that feeds you."

He typed in some more search words and scrolled through articles, information and sources for all the material. It was interesting stuff, not relevant to his writing, but she might get something out of the research. He printed out a list of topics then went back to his Mac Daniels file.

"What am I going to do with you?" he said to the blank screen, where his fictional character waited for a story. "You've been out of the military for a while and all you're good at is war and training for it. In the first book an old girlfriend sucked you into using those skills. You can handle yourself in a fight because you're trained to beat the crap out of bad guys. Now what?"

Except for the ex-girlfriend-rescue part that pretty much described himself, not Mac Daniels. Jack made a disgusted sound then leaned back in his chair. He was a piece of work, talking to himself. Well, not technically, since Harley was here, but too close for comfort. At least he knew his own flaws and keeping them to himself was the best way to control them.

There was a knock at the door then Erin poked her head in the room and smiled. "I'm back."

"Like the Terminator," he mumbled.

"I love that movie."

"Really?" He pegged her as more of a romantic-comedy type.

"Yes. You know romance is at the heart of the story."

"No pun intended."

She smiled. "What woman wouldn't want to hear, 'I came across time for you, Sarah.'"

Jack had never met a woman he'd want to time-travel for. But that was the best segue he could have hoped for. He pulled the sheet from his printer and held it out. "Your research topics."

"Right. I can't wait to get started." She took the paper and scanned it. To her credit, her perk factor only slipped a little.

The average person probably wouldn't have noticed. Jack was surprised that he had.

Her gaze settled on his and the vivid green was back. "The fine art of romantic talk?"

"Dialogue."

She glanced down at the paper. "A hundred and one ways to be romantic?"

"Mac spent a lot of time in a war zone." He shrugged as if to say that explained all.

"Understanding the female mind?"

"If he ever wants to get lucky, Mac might need some help."

There was a skeptical look on her face—she was suspicious and just a little annoyed. "These topics are important for an action-adventure book...why?"

Jack realized she'd already given him the answer to that question. "The Terminator effect."

"As it happens, women don't typically understand the male mind, either. I need more than that to connect the dots."

"You said you like the movie because there's a romance at the heart. It crosses genres and broadens the appeal."

"And?" One eyebrow rose.

"Maybe if Mac has a relationship it could expand my readership to women."

Her eyes narrowed and the I've-got-your-number look was back. "You don't fool me, Jack."

"I wasn't trying to." Did a half truth make something an out-and-out lie?

"Oh, please. This is you patting me on the head and telling me to run along."

"Not true."

"So in all of your own experience you've never sweet-talked a woman? Never made a romantic gesture? Or two?"

"Hard to say. I tried." With his ex-wife. But he didn't think she left him for lack of romance because she stayed for years while he went through numerous deployments. She left when he didn't re-up with the army. "But does a guy really know if he hit it out of the park with a woman?"

"You really don't know how to read people?"

"Hence the research for understanding the female mind," he pointed out.

She made a show of folding the paper and sticking it in the pocket of her jeans. "I'll do the research. But don't for a second believe that I don't know what you're up to. This is all about keeping me at a distance."

Jack didn't get a chance to respond because she turned and walked out of his office. Just as well. He needed to get to work. And she was wrong about his goal. The phony research wasn't to keep her at a distance, but to keep her in the dark about the fact that he didn't have a story. With luck he could fix the problem before she figured out what was going on.

The good news was that it was now quiet enough to work. And the bad news was he had to put some words on that blank page. And, damn it, he could still smell the scent of her skin. That brought to mind images of her smile and the fact that as hard as he'd tried to make her, she wouldn't back down from him.

Harley stood in his bed glancing from him to the door where Erin had exited. "Yeah, I know, buddy. I'm as surprised as you are that it's not so bad having her around for a distraction."

Chapter Three

In her new room Erin lay on her back trying to get to sleep, but the sound of pacing upstairs was distracting. So much for not waking her if he couldn't catch some z's and decided to work. Hard to type when you weren't sitting in front of a computer.

She was on the futon in the spare bedroom downstairs and it was surprisingly comfortable. That wasn't to blame for her restlessness; that was Jack's fault and not just on account of his walking back and forth, hitting that one squeaky board every time. Earlier he had opened the futon to make it flat and she'd been mesmerized by the play of muscles underneath the smooth material of his snug T-shirt.

Then she thought about one hundred and one ways to be romantic. Bring a woman flowers. Make her breakfast in bed. Surprise her with a B and B weekend. Picturing Jack doing any of those things made her smile. Forget romantic. He was barely civil.

A different sound caught her attention. The door to the

upstairs apartment closed and heavy footsteps sounded on the outside stairway. Erin tensed, waiting to hear him come inside. She could feel him when he was nearby and every cell in her body seemed to say "notice me." Which, of course, was never going to happen.

A few minutes passed and she still didn't hear him come inside. Wide-awake now, she tossed the sheet aside and turned on the light. The room was pretty big but had no personality. Unpacked boxes were stacked on the opposite wall. A lamp sat on what looked like an apple crate turned on end.

Erin grabbed the lightweight summer robe that matched her white cotton nightgown and slipped her arms into it. She pulled the pink satin tie tight around her waist, then let herself out of the room. It was time to find out if there was anything wrong. Then maybe she could get to sleep. One needed all of one's strength to deal with Jack Garner.

The house was dark and she felt for the hall switch to turn on the light. Brightness spilled into the empty living room. Cool air from outside washed over her and she realized that the front door was open. Looking through the screen, she saw Jack on the porch, staring out at the marina and Blackwater Lake beyond. She turned on the lights in the living room.

Barefoot, she walked outside and let the door close behind her. Between the lights and the screen door it was enough to guarantee he wouldn't be startled. "Is everything all right, Jack?"

He didn't flinch in surprise or bother to look over his shoulder for that matter. "Fine."

"It's late." Duh.

"Not for me."

She moved forward a couple of steps. Earlier when he'd asked her to move downstairs, she'd figured it was about keeping her away from his office space. The part about him working at night didn't ring true, but apparently she'd been wrong. "So you're up at night a lot?"

"Yeah." He finally turned to look at her. "You learn to sleep light, one eye open, waiting for something to happen."

"Doesn't sound restful."

"It's not." He slid his fingertips into the pockets of his worn jeans. "But you get used to functioning on little to no sleep."

"I suppose."

She could see a nearby full moon just above the dark silhouette of the mountains beyond the lake and there was a sky full of stars. The air was filled with the scent of pine and man, but she wasn't sure which was more intoxicating. One hundred and two ways to be romantic, she thought.

"Okay, then. I just wanted to make sure there was nothing wrong."

Before she could turn away, he asked, "Why aren't you asleep?"

Now wasn't that a valid question for which she had an embarrassment of answers. No way she'd confess to being distracted by his broad shoulders, muscular back and the romantic notions his research had stuck in her mind. And she didn't want him to feel bad about pacing. This was his home and moving around at night might be his creative process. She also didn't want to imply that moving downstairs had been a problem and make him feel guilty. But he'd already told her she was a bad liar.

So, she gave him the truth with a twist. "I was thinking."

His mouth curved into a slow, sexy smile. "Why doesn't that surprise me?"

"I don't know," she hedged. "Why doesn't it?"

"Because you're the kind of woman who thinks too much. Shakes things up."

"In a good way? Or bad?"

"Both," he said.

She had a feeling he wasn't just talking about the job she was sent here to do. That maybe he was hinting at something a little more personal. The thought made her heart race and she had to stop herself from pressing fingertips to the pounding pulse at the base of her throat. He'd know why and that would show him her vulnerability and give him more of an upper hand than he already had.

"I've been thinking about you." Oh, dear God, that was no better and she desperately wanted the words back.

"Oh?"

She saw the gleam in his eyes and felt a shiver clear to her bare toes. "Now that I have your attention—" She drew in a breath. "What I meant was, I've been thinking about what the military must have been like."

"Civilians don't have a clue."

"You're right, of course. But there are basics. You're expected to follow orders."

"From a commanding officer," he pointed out.

"Right. I'm not giving orders. But I was getting at the discipline factor. You're told where to go, when to report for duty and what job to do."

"Chain of command is followed," he admitted. "If not there would be chaos in the ranks."

"In civilian life we call it a schedule."

The look on his face said he was bracing himself for whatever she had in mind. "What's your point?"

"A schedule."

He moved his shoulders as if they'd tensed up, then stared at her for several moments. "Oh, you mean me."

"Actually I mean both of us." She curled her toes into

the wooden porch. "You had discipline in the military and it would behoove you to establish that in your writing life."

One corner of his mouth quirked up. "Who says *be-hoove* in actual conversation?"

"An English teacher."

"Right." He folded his arms over his chest. "What did you have in mind?"

"Breakfast first. Your mind and body need fuel." She had not expected him to be even this receptive. "Then we meet in your office for a…let's call it a status meeting. We discuss what you're going to work on and you can give me a list of research topics for anything necessary for the story. Think of it as punching a time clock."

"Don't tell me. This status meeting would be at nine in the morning."

"Yes. How did you know?"

"Just a guess."

"So, what do you think of the idea?"

"Do you really want to know?" he asked.

"Of course. This needs to work for you. It's all about fine-tuning your process. You're the author." She watched him watch her, his gaze flicking over her body, and wished she was wearing jeans and a big, bulky sweatshirt. A thin cotton nightgown and matching robe came under the heading of Didn't Think It Through. Where was a girl's body armor when she really needed it? "Sometimes it's just about putting your butt in the chair. Sheer boredom will force you into doing something."

"Doing something—" His voice was husky, deeper than normal.

Erin sensed tension in him but had a feeling it wasn't about her suggestions for his work schedule. "Anyway, that's what I was thinking about. Give it some thought and let me know in the morning—"

"Okay."

She blinked. "What?"

"Permission granted. We'll try it your way."

"That's great, Jack." She was oddly happy that he'd actually listened to her. "Thank you for meeting me halfway on this."

"This isn't halfway," he said, staring at her. "It's damn near all the way."

"What? I don't understand—"

"For the record, it's not fair to dress like that when you're asking for something." There was a ragged edge to his voice and his gaze never left her.

"There's nothing wrong with what I'm wearing." That was sheer bravado since moments ago she'd wished for body armor. Then she looked down at the eyelet cotton robe with pink accents and her cheeks suddenly burned with mortification. She realized that with the light behind her, the material was nearly transparent. "Oh, God—"

"Yeah." A muscle jerked in his jaw.

Erin's knees got weak and that was a first. No man had ever made her weak in the knees before. "I'm going in now. You should get some sleep."

"Right."

There was a mother lode of sarcasm in the single word, yet she felt it like a caress that touched her everywhere. The look in his eyes sharpened her senses and she tingled in places that might not have ever tingled before.

"Good night, Jack." She tried to make her voice decisive, authoritative, unwavering, but was afraid the words came out weak, wishy-washy and just the tiniest bit wanton.

With all the dignity she could muster, Erin backed up to the door then quickly turned and opened it. She went to her room and shut herself in, then sagged against the door.

"What just happened?" she whispered.

There had been a moment. She was sure of it. Until just a few minutes ago, no man had ever looked at her as if he wanted her more than his next breath. Not even the man she'd taken an engagement ring from. But Jack Garner did.

She didn't know whether to high-five herself or crawl into bed and pull the covers over her head. Then an even more off-putting thought struck her. Was that the way she'd looked at him when they first met? When he'd said they weren't sleeping together as if that's what she'd been thinking.

How was she going to face him tomorrow morning?

Jack sat across from Erin at the kitchen table and finished his omelet. It was becoming clear that she was very good at making them. Spinach, tomatoes, mushrooms and cheese—he couldn't say he'd ever had a better one. The eggs were fluffy and filling. The company…not so much. Since he'd come downstairs for breakfast, the cook had barely looked at him.

Barely was most probably the reason why.

She'd been practically naked on the porch last night and his gut still hurt from the effort it took to keep his hands to himself. The high color in her cheeks was a clue that she was still embarrassed about it. She'd admitted to having a long-term relationship, but there was an innocence about her that was inconvenient. Since coming downstairs for breakfast he hadn't done anything except eat. There had been nothing to take the edge off the tension. If he left it alone and let her feel uncomfortable, maybe she would take off back where she came from.

He sneaked a look and there was something sweet and vulnerable about her that made him feel like a buffalo at a tea party. Damn it. Probably he was going to regret this, but…

"Breakfast was good." There, silence broken.

Erin stopped pushing the food around her plate without eating it and looked at him. "Really?"

"Yeah. Coffee's good, too."

"Thanks, I'm glad you liked it. Some guys think vegetable omelets aren't very…well, masculine."

"What guy?"

"My fiancé."

Jack bit his tongue to keep from saying this fiancé was an idiot. Not only was it bad to speak ill of the dead, but a remark like that would also undermine what he was trying to do in erasing her embarrassment. All he said was "His loss."

"That's nice of you to say, Jack."

"Not really. I'm not a nice guy. It's just the truth."

Whatever else he was, wasn't, or had done, he always tried to be honest. Mostly he was successful, but probably not always. "You're a good cook."

"It's just something I like to do. Guess that's half the battle. When I was a little girl, I stayed with my grandmother a lot because my mom worked. Grammy let me help when she cooked or baked. I got to roll out dough, cut out cookies and help make soup." There was a faraway look in her eyes and the corners of her mouth curved up in a small smile. "Those are good memories."

"I never knew my grandmother." Now, why the hell had he said that?

"Singular? You only had one parent?"

He looked at her for a long moment, kicking himself for going soft and letting that out. It was too much to hope she'd miss the slipup. "Obviously at a certain point I had a father, but he was nothing more than a sperm donor."

"You never met him?"

The pity in her eyes made him want to put his fist

through a wall. "She always said he was a magician. When he heard my mother say the word *pregnant*, he made himself disappear."

"I don't know what to say."

"That's a first. But if you feel compelled to comment, just don't say you're sorry. I never needed him." Jack learned a code of honor in the military and did his best to be honest, but that statement closed in on the line that separated truth from deceit.

"You are many things, Jack, but I would never describe you as someone to be pitied." Then she pointed a warning finger at him. "And don't tell me I'm patronizing you because I'm not doing that."

Since that's exactly what he'd been about to say, he almost smiled but caught himself just in time. That was annoying, one more way she tempted him. Enough of this. After pushing his chair back from the table, he said, "I have to get to work."

She glanced at the funky pink princess watch on her wrist. "Oh, wow. It's getting late."

Only if one was on a schedule, which he'd agreed to in a weak moment when he'd been unable to look away from her practically naked body. "Yeah. It's closing right in on nine."

"I'll clean up the kitchen."

Jack knew he should offer to help but this time was able to hold back the words. Washing dishes with her was domestic and he didn't do domestic. Not anymore.

Without another word he walked to the front door and Harley followed from wherever he'd been dozing. They went out onto the porch then up the stairs to his office.

Jack sat down in the chair behind his desk and looked at the blank computer monitor for a while. He patted his leg and said, "Harley, up."

The dog did as ordered then made a circle before settling on Jack's lap. He scratched the animal's hairless back and hoped the mindless activity would stimulate something creative or useful. Ten minutes later he still had nothing.

There was a knock on his office door before Erin stuck her head inside. "Rough commute. Am I late?"

If only. "Nine o'clock on the nose." Damn it.

She took a seat in front of the desk. "Okay, let the status meeting begin. Where are you in the book?"

"Where am I?" he repeated. Harley chose that moment to desert him and jump down and pad over to her. "Well, let me think. That's kind of hard to say."

"Yeah. I can see where it would be. Why don't you start by telling me what you have so far."

"What I have… Let's see." He leaned back in his chair and linked his fingers over his abdomen. "Wow. Where do I begin…?"

Really, he wanted to say. *Where?* Did he open the story with unknown assailants ambushing Mac and leaving him for dead? Or with a mysterious stranger who contacts him for help because word of his exploits in rescuing the ex-girlfriend's kidnapped kid from a vicious drug cartel had spread? The best first line would be something like "The pretty, green-eyed woman with sun-streaked brown hair smiled seductively before telling him to forget the book and take her to bed."

Erin waited patiently for him to speak. When the silence drifted into awkward territory she said, "You know, Corinne Carlisle had a hard time talking about her story, too. It could be an author thing because you're more comfortable with the written word than the spoken one."

Helpful of her to gift-wrap an excuse for him. "Yeah, I think you just nailed it."

"Are you a pantser or a plotter?" she asked.

"I have no idea what you're talking about."

"Do you write by the seat of your pants? Or do you know every detail ahead of time when you sit down at the computer?"

Right this minute he wished to be a plotter but was pretty sure the first one described him best. "That's really hard to say."

"Okay." She nodded thoughtfully. "Then let's talk about your characters."

Oh, boy. He could really use an interruption about now. A phone call, package delivery, or a little rocket attack. "The thing is, I don't have all the characters set in stone yet. Still trying to flesh them out."

"You have Mac," she pointed out.

Good old Mac. "I do have him."

"What's happened to him in the time since we left him at the end of book one?"

"That's a good question. I'm glad you asked." Not.

She waited for him to elaborate. So it was safe to say she wasn't an interrupter. Boy, did he wish she was.

"So," Jack said. "He's been kicking around."

"In Los Angeles? Or has he gone to Dallas, Topeka, or Micronesia?" The perky, trying-to-be-helpful tone was missing in action from her voice.

"He hasn't moved." And that was Jack's fault because he hadn't moved his main character.

"In the last book he had just left the army and had no plan for his life before being pulled into that case involving his dead buddy's younger brother, who was married to his ex-girlfriend."

"Yeah." Funny how the no-plan-for-his-life part sounded a lot like Jack.

"How is he supporting himself?"

"Odd jobs. This and that." And in a military operation

when you wanted to avoid direct confrontation with an enemy that had superior firepower, a good soldier created a diversion. He took a piece of paper from the printer tray beside him. "I put together some things for you to research."

Erin's eyes narrowed as she took it from him, then scanned the list. "Meteors? Dinosaurs?" She met his gaze. "You probably already know that *Jurassic Park* has been done." She looked down again. "Jet Skis?"

"All things I'm considering incorporating into the story."

With careful, precise movements she folded the single sheet several times before slicing him with a look. "What's going on, Jack?"

"I need you to look stuff up."

"No, you don't. You're trying to distract me and it's time for you to cut the crap."

"Is that any way to talk to your employer?"

"Technically I work for the publishing house, specifically your editor. So, yeah, it's a very good way to address a man who is not forthcoming."

"What makes you think something's going on?" Besides the fact that he kept dodging her direct questions?

"Classic avoidance. And to quote Shakespeare—'let me count the ways.'" She held up her fingers. "You won't talk about the story, characters or what your hero has been doing. I'm pretty sure that means you have no idea. And every time I push for information, you come up with a distraction. Some ridiculous research stuff that has nothing to do with your genre. One hundred and one ways to be romantic—really, Jack? You even threw me out of my room and kicked me downstairs." She took a breath. "So call me paranoid and neurotic—"

"Don't forget punctual," he added helpfully.

"—but I'm suspicious," she continued without missing

a beat after his interjection. "Your editor would welcome an outline of the project. Not details, necessarily, just the beginning, middle and end of the story. Possibly a one-line characterization of the hero."

Jack met her gaze, stare for stare. Her perky, cheerful interrogation might have given him a sense of her being a pushover. Now he saw the error of that assumption. She was sunshine and steel.

Still, he couldn't resist trying one more time. "There's nothing to be suspicious about. I'm in the process of pulling all the threads together."

"Then let me see your pages." She suddenly stood and moved around the desk to look at his computer monitor. "It's not even turned on."

"That's easy to rectify."

"Okay. Let me see the work you've done so far."

This time Jack did squirm, and Harley had disappeared down the hall so there was no way to keep Erin from noticing. "The work needs editing—"

She held up a hand. "There's something wrong and I want to know what it is. I'm here to help you finish this manuscript and I can't if you're hiding something."

Her relentless questions were like water dripping on a stone, wearing away the outer protection. Jack was at a crossroads. He knew what it looked like because he'd seen it before in the heat of battle when there was no wiggle room left. Almost always a course of action revealed itself and this situation was no different. Her counteroffensive left him no choice. He had to tell the truth or lie to her and he couldn't do that.

"So quit stalling and turn on the monitor, Jack. Let me see your work."

"I haven't started it."

"Of course not today. The laptop isn't even on yet. I want to see what you've got so far," she stressed.

"You don't understand." He met her gaze.

"Then enlighten me."

"I have nothing. There is no book."

Chapter Four

Erin blinked several times, letting the words sink in, while slowly lowering herself into the chair. "What do you mean there's no book? What do you do up here all day?"

"I write pages. Every single day. Then I delete them because they're all crap."

Oh God. Oh God. Oh God. The chant went through her mind as she desperately tried to think of something helpful to say. "Is everything deleted?"

"I have about twenty pages."

"Let me see them." Was her voice even and unemotional? She hoped it didn't show the panic that was slowly creeping in as the magnitude of this situation became clear.

Jack turned on the computer and pulled up a file, then hit the print button. When the last page came out he handed them to her.

Erin started reading and with the turn of every page her heart sank a little more. There was nothing wrong with the writing and there was a wry, masculine voice to the work, but it was all internal dialogue from Mac Daniels's point of view. Nothing particularly exciting was going on. Quite frankly there was a very high boredom factor but no way could she tell him that. His instincts, however, were right about the quality of these pages.

She looked up and met his gaze. "I have to agree with you. This isn't your best work."

"Since you showed up we've disagreed on almost everything. I was hoping that streak would continue." His mouth pulled tight for a moment, then he rubbed Harley's head when the dog jumped back into his lap and looked at him. The animal apparently felt his tension. "So you think it's crap, too."

"I didn't say that. Don't panic."

Jack looked the opposite of panicked—cool, calm collected. And she needed to be that way, too. This was why she was here. But she needed to think.

"I'm going for a walk."

Instantly Harley jumped off Jack's lap and began to whine. "Now you've done it."

"What?"

"You said the *w* word. If you're not prepared to take him it's best to spell. *W-a-l-k*." There was amusement in his eyes. "There's very little he likes better. Except maybe raw hamburger. But the *w* is in his top two."

"Sorry. I won't make that mistake again." She headed for the door, wincing at the sounds of doggy protest behind her.

After going outside, the yelping got worse as she hurried down the stairs. Moments later she heard the door open and in seconds the dog was happily dancing at her feet. He ran several yards away then came back, repeating the exercise several more times.

"You're not subtle, Harley." She looked at Jack, who'd come up beside her. "Neither are you."

"I think that's the nicest thing you've ever said to me, Miss Riley."

Instead of rising to the bait, she decided to comment on the fact that it wasn't his usual time to walk and he'd given in to Harley. "You know you're spoiling that dog."

He met her gaze and shrugged. He was either avoiding work or didn't care. "Harley, walk."

Jack started after the dog, who instantly ran down the path that skirted the lake. She stared at his back, the man's, admiring his broad shoulders and muscular back that tapered to a trim waist and really nice butt, wrapped with just the perfect amount of snugness in worn denim. How the heck had those two hijacked her walk?

She could go in the opposite direction but since the whole purpose of her being here was to get his book finished, probably talking to him would be a good idea. Even though she was furious.

His long legs had chewed up a fair amount of distance by the time she'd made up her mind and she hurried to catch up. When that happened, she fell into step beside him. Her mind was spinning from his revelation and she needed to organize her thoughts. If she'd been alone that wouldn't be a challenge, but the manly scent of his skin combined with the smell of pine effectively made thinking difficult.

Apparently Jack didn't have any thoughts to organize because after a few moments he said, "You're uncharacteristically quiet."

"I didn't think you paid enough attention to me to know what's characteristic for me."

"In the army you learn pretty fast that paying attention to your surroundings means survival."

"And you see me as a threat to that?" She was being petulant. He could just sue her.

"Not my personal safety, no."

"Then you think your way of life is at risk by my being here? You're wrong, Jack. I'm only trying to help you." As they walked she met his gaze and tripped over the uneven ground. Instantly he grabbed her arm to steady her. Being touched by him easily scattered the few thoughts she'd managed to gather. She mumbled under her breath, "Pigheaded...stubborn—"

"Harley—" At his voice, the dog turned and headed back. "I heard that."

"Ask me if I care."

"Let me take a wild guess. You're mad."

"Give the man a prize." She refused to look at him and only heard the surprise in his voice. "I am so ticked off. You have wasted so much time. Why in the world didn't you say something when I first got here? When I tried to have a conversation about what was going on? You had numerous opportunities to come clean, yet you shut me out. Why?"

When Harley sniffed at his boots, Jack squatted down and rubbed his head. He looked up and said, "Because I'm used to being the guy who's inserted into a hot zone to fix whatever is wrong."

Holding her breath, Erin waited for him to say more. When he didn't, she figured that was as close as he'd get to admitting he wasn't used to needing or asking for help. She sensed he almost never did it and the fact that he had took all the irritation out of her. Or maybe she was just a pushover because of her acute attraction to him, but that didn't change anything. There was a problem and they had to find a way to fix it.

"Okay, we know you can write a successful book. You

wrote a bestseller." She knew she'd hit a nerve when his jaw tensed and a muscle jerked. "There's no reason you can't do it again."

"Says who? Maybe I only had one book in me." He watched Harley sniff the side of the path then pick up a stick, which he dropped at Jack's feet. He picked it up and threw it as far as he could.

"Your creativity just needs a jump start."

He tilted his head and looked at her. "What happened to if you stared at a blank screen long enough you'll get bored and write something on it?"

"I did say that." She thought for a moment. "But it helps if you know what you're going to write."

He snorted. "Are you going to give me the pantsers-and-plotters speech again?"

"That was a definition, not a speech. But I'll remind you what I said about talking out the plot. Discussing the hero's goals. His mind-set since we last saw him."

"Any thoughts on that?" He all but growled those words, as if his asking-for-assistance muscles were rusty.

"Yes. But feel free to tell me I'm full of it. The point is to toss out ideas and see what feels right in your gut." She slid her fingertips into the pockets of her jeans. "Mac had no emotional growth in the first book because he went into fight-or-flight mode almost right away."

"So he's still aimless."

"Right. Unless he's independently wealthy, he has to have been thinking about what he'll do to support himself since leaving the military." Her mind was spinning. "Come to think of it, we don't really know why he left. He was a career soldier and his reasoning could be explored in this book."

Jack nodded absently. "Yeah."

That was encouraging, she thought. An affirmative instead of sarcasm. She dipped her toe in a little further. "When we get back, it might help to just talk it through and you could take notes. Or record the conversation if you'd rather. Instead of jumping straight into the writing, you can figure out the inciting incident that sets the story in motion, then some loose turning points as a structure for the story."

"And tomorrow there will still be a blank screen."

"Give yourself permission to write badly," she suggested.

His look was wry. "Yeah, because that's what I learned in the army. Permission to be a screwup, sir."

"Maybe it sounds crazy, but you might find it surprisingly freeing."

"And that's supposed to be creative?" he asked skeptically.

"Won't know unless you try." She thought for a moment. "Some authors start their day by jotting down stream-of-consciousness writing."

"You mean gibberish?"

"Probably not something you'd publish," she admitted.

"Then I guess you could say I've already done that. The pages you read are unpublishable and probably fall into the stream-of-consciousness category," he said sarcastically.

"That's not what I meant. You just write whatever pops into your mind," she explained.

"Sounds like a waste of time if you ask me."

"It's just an exercise."

Erin glanced up at him and felt a little flutter around her heart, the one that made it hard to take a deep breath. The way his biceps strained against the material of his black T-shirt made her want to touch and find out for herself what they felt like.

It was obvious that Jack was in excellent physical condition, which meant he'd retained habits from his time in the army that kept him in shape. She knew he ran three or four times a week. There was workout equipment in the upstairs bedroom. One didn't just jump into a fitness regime. Maybe she could explain this to him in a relatable way.

"What do you do before a run?" she asked.

His gaze narrowed on her. "Why?"

"Bear with me. I have a point." Their shoulders brushed as they walked. Personally she was glad the bushes and trees around them weren't tinder-dry because the sparks would have ignited them. She drew in a breath. "What's your preexercise routine?"

"I stretch out. Warm up."

"Exactly."

He looked at her as if she had a snake draped around her neck. "I thought you had a point."

"Stream-of-consciousness writing is like stretching your muscles for work."

"Shouldn't I put that energy into something productive?"

"The point is to not think about work. Free your mind and let the ideas flow."

His expression was still skeptical, but he asked, "What should I write about?"

"Like I said. Anything that pops into your mind."

Jack looked down at the dog, who had thrown himself on the ground at his feet. Automatically he picked up the animal and rubbed his hand over the hairless back. "I still say it's a waste of time."

This man was results-driven. He'd spent over a decade in an organized, mission-oriented environment. The creative process was the polar opposite. But if she could give him a focus, he might be more inclined to give it a try.

As they headed back to the house, she watched him with

the dog. His protectiveness with the animal. The way he automatically picked up Harley when he got tired. Jack had done the same thing that first day when she'd arrived. There was a bond between the two and that homely little creature might just be what he cared about most in this world.

"Write about Harley," she suggested.

"What?"

"Stream-of-consciousness warm-up exercises. Think about your dog and jot down whatever comes into your mind."

With the dog curled happily in his arms, Jack stared at her for several moments. She wondered how it would feel to be safely tucked against his wide chest, wrapped in his strong arms.

Then he shook his head. "It's official. You're crazy."

About you, she thought.

For a moment Erin was afraid she'd said that out loud. Fortunately, the words stayed in her head, where they belonged. He already knew she was attracted to him. If she confirmed it he would say I told you so and send her packing.

Erin didn't want to get out of bed after a lousy night without much sleep. And that was all Jack's fault. He was a bundle of contrasts. Gruff and argumentative with her; tender and protective of his unattractive pet. He measured out a quarter cup of organic chicken or grass-fed beef for Harley's meals! He was a really off-putting combination of macho and mush.

And she knew very little about him. Was there a girlfriend? Wife? But those questions fell into personal territory, which technically made it not her business. And don't even get her started on the geographical situation here. Last night she'd heard him pacing like a predatory tiger.

Back and forth. Back and forth. At least an hour. Maybe more.

Then it got quiet and she'd waited for him to come downstairs to bed. That kept her tense and wide-eyed for a long time. Her body tingled and her skin was hot whenever he was in the master bedroom just across the hall from where she slept. She would challenge anyone to try sleeping when every nerve ending was sparking like a live electrical wire.

After starting a reread of his bestselling book, she finally fell asleep sometime after one o'clock. Now it was six in the morning. Soon she'd need to start breakfast, then meet Jack at nine in his office. If she hauled her hiney out of bed there was just enough time to get in some yoga. Maybe some flexibility poses would flex thoughts of the difficult man out of her mind.

She put on her nylon-and-spandex capris and the stretchy, racer-back tank top she wore for workouts, then rolled out her mat. Mountain pose was first. Standing straight, heels down, shoulders directly over hips. Breathe. Then raised arms. Grounded in her heels, shoulders away from ears and reaching through her fingertips. She held that for the required time and went into the standing forward bend. Exhale and fold down over legs. Let head hang heavy with feet hip distance apart. That was followed by the garland pose, which she hated.

For the lunge pose she started with the right leg forward and the left straight and strong, the heel reaching. She repeated switching legs. About an hour later she'd gone through her routine and worked up a sweat. She rolled up her yoga mat and stood it in the corner next to the unpacked boxes stacked there.

After leaving her room she listened for sounds of Jack and heard none. His bedroom door was opened, meaning he wasn't there, and she thought he'd either slept upstairs or gone for an early morning run. In the kitchen she pulled a bottle of water from the refrigerator and started to twist off the top when she heard the front door open and close.

Jack walked into the room and his shorts and sweaty gray T-shirt told her she'd been right about the run. He looked her over from head to toe and there was a dark sort of intensity in his eyes.

Erin felt the power of that look slip deep inside, tapping into a place where she wanted to be just a tiny bit wicked. He didn't even have to say a word to make her respond to him. When she felt as if she could speak without stammering, she said, "Do you want water?"

"Yeah."

She opened the refrigerator and pulled out a bottle, then handed it to him. "So, *exercise* is the word of the day."

"Apparently."

"Do you want coffee? I was just about to make a pot."

"Affirmative."

"Okay."

She turned away to start the process and resisted the urge to look over her shoulder. The thing was, it didn't matter whether or not she looked. He was *there*. Right on cue her nerves started that electrical arcing thing. Her hands shook as she performed the familiar, ordinary task of filling the coffeemaker reservoir with water and measuring grounds into a filter. Then she pushed the power button and heard the heating element start to sizzle. Or was that her? It was hard to tell if she was hot all over from yoga or Jack's scorching look.

She turned to face him and instantly his gaze lifted to her face. It wasn't possible to be sure he'd been staring at her butt, although the look in his eyes had turned smoky and a muscle jerked in his jaw. That was the same expression he'd worn when she stood on the porch in her cotton nightgown with the light making it practically see-through. Her exercise clothes stretched over her body like a second skin. Did he like what he saw?

She had to break the silence and said the first thing that popped into her mind. "So, I heard you pacing last night."

"Yeah. It helps me think." He leaned a broad shoulder against the wall just inside the doorway.

"Do you want to talk about it?"

"Thinking?" One corner of his mouth quirked up, softening the hard lines of his face. "It just sort of happens on its own."

She folded her arms over her chest. "Would it kill you to answer a question in a serious, straightforward way?"

"It might." He lifted a shoulder in a shrug.

"Well, from what I heard there must have been a lot of thinking going on. That made me wonder if you might have had a breakthrough to discuss. I'm happy to talk about it."

"You're a good talker. I've noticed that about you."

"And you're not."

Right behind her the coffee continued dripping into the pot and the warm, cozy aroma of it filled the room. If anyone saw them now, they could be mistaken for a couple starting out their day. Which they were, but not as a couple. He looked as if sleep had been hard to come by. There were lines on either side of his nose that were signs of fatigue and a supersexy dark scruff on his jaw. Her palms tingled with the urge to brush her hands over his face.

Finally he said, "There's not much to say."

"I disagree. I've told you practically everything about me, but you're a mystery."

"You know all there is to know about me."

"Hardly." She glanced around the kitchen. It was functional, serviceable, but without any cozy pictures or touches that were evidence of this being a home. "I know that you wrote a bestselling action-adventure book. You were a member of army Special Forces, Ranger Battalion. And you have a weakness for strange-looking dogs."

The dog in question padded into the room and looked at his dish then up at Jack. Staring at the animal he said, "What do you want to know?"

"Do you have a girlfriend?"

"No."

"Are you married?"

"No." But something flashed in his eyes. Anger? Hurt? Regret?

"Does that mean you're not married now? Or that you've never been married? Because you know what they say about a man your age who's never been married." She shrugged, hoping he would fill in for her.

"My age?" One dark eyebrow rose.

"Seriously? That's what you got from what I just said?"

"You implied I'm old."

She shook her head. "Either you're deliberately missing the point or you're dense as dirt."

"I don't think so. You specifically said a man of my age."

"Who's never been married," she reminded him.

"What do they say?" he asked, suddenly pretending to be interested.

"That there's something really wrong." She had the sense that he was enjoying baiting her. "You know what I think? You're focusing on minutiae to avoid answering my question."

"You could Google me."

"I have."

"Should I be flattered that you went through the trouble?" He was laughing at her.

"Trouble? That I was trying to find out more about you because we're working together? Or the fact that you've quite successfully managed to not reveal any personal information for public consumption?"

He moved farther into the room and leaned his back against the granite-topped island. "Why do you want personal information?"

"I just do." She wasn't going to tell him it was because she needed a good reason to put the brakes on this crush she had going on. Plus, the more he dodged, the more determined she was to get the truth. "So, have you ever been married? What possible reason could you have to avoid answering that question?"

"I'm a private person."

"You used to be but not anymore. Not since your book hit the bestseller lists and stayed there."

"Drip, drip, drip," he said.

"What does that mean?"

"You're like water on a rock, wearing it down."

She lifted her chin. "I like to think that's one of my best qualities."

"It's good." Jack's gaze dropped to her chest and the glitter was back in his eyes. "But not your best."

He didn't miss much so she was pretty sure he could tell that the pulse in her neck had just gone from normal to racing. There was only one way to interpret those words and that look. He moved closer and she held her breath, hoping that he was going to kiss her. Heat from his body warmed her skin when he stopped right in front of her.

Their shoulders brushed and gazes locked. Sexual tension crackled in the air between them and seemed to push the pause button on everything around them. Was it now? Surely he would touch his mouth to hers now.

Then he looked up and over her head, shattering the moment. He reached into the cupboard behind her and said, "Do you want coffee?"

Erin blinked and managed to answer in the affirmative, but for as long as she lived she would never know how she did it. She stepped sideways and let him get out mugs and pour coffee into them.

Mug in hand, he headed for the doorway. It was as if that click between them had never happened. "I'm going to take a shower."

"I'll start breakfast."

"Good. I'm starved." He stopped and sent a look over his shoulder.

Then he was gone and Erin could breathe again. If anything positive had come out of what just happened, it was that she had a little bit more information about him. No girlfriend and no marriage meant he was single. A bachelor. Available. And he hadn't taken advantage of the opportunity to kiss her. There was only one conclusion to draw. He wasn't interested in her.

Maybe thinking he was attracted had been her imagination. All her concentration on the writing process had her subconscious creating character motivation where there was none. But tell that to female hormones all revved up with no place to go.

From now on she was going to dress like a bag lady. *That* was her best quality.

Chapter Five

After breakfast Jack went to his office and sat behind his desk while the clock ticked ever closer to the 9:00 a.m. status meeting. The truth was that his status was tipping into chaos and confusion. When he saw Erin in those workout clothes, he felt as if he'd been sucker punched. The tight pants left almost nothing to the imagination.

It was the *almost* that really tied him in knots because he didn't want to imagine. Erin Riley was trim, taut and tempting. More than almost anything he wanted to touch her bare skin and taste it, too. And *take* her—

There was a knock on the door and he braced himself for her pert and perky personality. "Come in."

She did and assumed her position in the chair facing his desk. "Ready to get to work?"

"Raring to go." And work had nothing to do with it.

"Okay. Let's talk about the book."

"Is it really necessary to remind you that there is no book?"

"I meant the already published one," she amended.

Geez, he never knew what to expect from her. One minute she was innocent and vulnerable, the next showing off curves that would test the willpower of a man trained to resist even the most aggressive interrogation techniques. She kept him off balance and he didn't like being off balance. Any more than he liked her attempt to find out personal information. What in the world had made him tell her to ask whatever she wanted to know? He regretted that as much as seeing her in those skintight yoga clothes.

"Jack?"

"Hmm?"

"Are you with me?"

"Yeah." He sat forward and rested his forearms on the desk. "I just don't see how discussing *High Value Target* is going to help with this book."

"You never know what will trigger a creative leap forward."

Since he had nothing to show for all the time he'd put in, what did he have to lose? "Okay. What about it?"

"I reread the book."

"Why?"

"Besides the fact that I was having trouble sleeping—"

"Wait." He held up a hand to stop her right there. "You thought my book would put you to sleep?"

"Of course not. I was just trying to put that awake time to good use. And I really enjoyed it the first time, Jack."

"Then why the second read?"

"For ideas."

"And?" he persisted.

"Let me tell you what I did and didn't like."

That got his full attention. "There was something you didn't like?"

"I'm a tough crowd. An English teacher always is." She

shrugged. "Critiquing requires a delicate balance. It's just as important to highlight what works as what doesn't."

"Okay. What did you like?"

"The hero."

It was hard to keep from grinning. Jack had based Mac Daniels on himself. After retiring from the military he'd read that journaling helped put into perspective things you were trying not to think about. That's how the book had started in the first place. For Ms. Tough Crowd to like *him* felt damn good.

"So, you think Mac works."

"Incredibly well," she said. "Men want to be him and women want to be with him. That's why there's such cross-over appeal and the book did so well."

This critique thing wasn't so bad after all. "What else did you like?"

"The action was realistic and suspenseful. It makes the reader feel right there—in the moment. When Mac slaps another magazine into his pistol, you can practically hear the sound of it."

Jack didn't have to hear it; he would never forget that distinctive sound. "Good."

"Clearly you know your protagonist and his strengths. Also his weaknesses. It's incredibly appealing that he's well-rounded. But—" She crossed one leg over the other, apparently pulling her thoughts together.

The movement completely destroyed his ability to think clearly. He couldn't seem to take his eyes off her legs. Or eject the image of black spandex outlining the luscious curves and tanned skin of her calves just before he took off those tight pants and she wrapped her legs around his waist.

If his editor had really wanted him to concentrate on the project, she could have sent someone older. And not pretty. Better yet, a guy. How was he supposed to concentrate when all he wanted to do was leap over the desk and kiss Erin? He was feeling creative, all right, but it had nothing to do with writing his book and everything to do with what they could accomplish in the sack.

"Since you didn't ask, I guess you don't want to hear the *but*," she said.

"No one ever wants to hear the *but*. Worst word in the English language. It always goes something like this. 'Everything's fine, but you lost your job. The decor is beautiful, but the food sucks. You're going to live, but the leg has to be amputated.' No one wants to know what comes after the *but*. Guaranteed you're not going to like it."

"You're right. Of course. And remember this is only my opinion."

"But—" He filled that word with as much sarcasm as possible.

"Mac is well-defined and the action is compelling and believable. But the secondary characters are one-dimensional, a little clichéd. Take the villain—"

"I did. Or Mac did. Took him right out."

"Fairly spectacularly, too. But the guy was all evil weasel with no redeeming qualities. No one, even the bad guys, is that simple. They had parents, possibly siblings or significant others. Children. All of that shapes them into the person they are."

Although Jack didn't want to admit it, she had a point. In war it was more black-and-white. You took out the guy trying to take you out. Survival. As simple as that.

"Okay."

"And remember, the hero is only as heroic as the adversary he faces."

"So the stronger and more formidable the bad guy, the better Mac looks."

"Exactly."

The smile she gave him was like a slice of sunlight riding a rainbow straight through him. "Good point."

"Real people have flaws, a gray area. They're human. The baddie might be completely in love with an innocent, vulnerable woman yet he can do despicable things." Harley stood, got out of his bed and walked over to her. She reached down and scratched his head, then laughed when he rolled onto his back and exposed his belly to be rubbed. "Could be that he has a soft spot for animals."

"Or the villain is a woman." He had a lot of material from his ex to channel into a character like that.

"Speaking of women—" She stopped and met his gaze. "There wasn't a real woman in the story."

"How can you say that?"

"They were either like robots, completely unemotional and too sticky sweet. Or overly emotional and hysterical. There was no middle ground."

"Give me a for-instance," he said defensively.

"Okay." She thought for a moment. "Got one. When Mac breaks up with Karen, who's been waiting for him to come home from Afghanistan, and she starts punching and slapping him, that seemed out of character for someone who'd been so patient."

"She was ticked off at being dumped. But he didn't want to lead her on."

"And rightfully so. But because she was so long-suffering and colorless it didn't feel real."

"What would have been right? In your opinion," he said defensively. In his case, he'd been the one dumped and the only blows had been on the inside, where they wouldn't show.

"She might cry. Struggle to hold back tears. Try to talk

him out of it. Or let him have it with words. But she probably wouldn't attack him physically."

He wasn't ready yet to concede the point even though his gut was telling him she was right. "It could happen."

"But probably not." She gave him a wry look. "Your response makes me wonder if you have issues with women."

"What are you talking about?"

"Maybe you don't like them."

"I like women just fine." And that was the truth. But he wasn't very good with them. If he was, he'd have sensed his wife's detachment before she made the distance real and permanent.

"All I know is that you don't have a girlfriend and you're not married. Maybe you're gay."

"I'm not."

"And in denial," she said.

Just a little while ago he'd taken the high road and passed up the opportunity to show her he liked women just fine. But during that second or two in the kitchen, when he'd reached into the cupboard for a mug, he'd accidentally brushed against her. That barest of touches had sent his blood rushing to points south of his belt.

In spite of what she thought, he knew a little something about women. He knew when one would melt against him if he kissed her. And that's exactly the way Erin had looked in that moment when their bodies had touched.

"I know exactly who I am," he said. "And I don't have issues with women."

"If you need help with the female point of view, I'd be happy to provide feedback."

"I don't need help understanding women."

"Really? Then you would be the first man in history who didn't," she said pertly. "Look, Jack, all I'm saying is that you can make your characters do whatever you need them to, just give them a backstory to support the behavior. Readers want real characters, get to know and root for them."

"Understood."

"Maybe Mac Daniels needs a love interest. A woman, or man," she said with a grin, "who will tell him the things he really doesn't want to hear. Someone to keep him honest. Because right now he really has nothing to lose and it means the stakes for him are pretty low."

"I need to get to work." He took a sheet of paper from the printer. "And I have some serious things for you to research."

"Right." She stood and took the paper. "Later, Jack."

He watched the sway of her hips as she walked to the door and didn't realize he was holding his breath until she was gone and he let it out.

Had she been pushing his buttons to get him to open up?

Off balance. There it was again. And he had another reason to regret missing the opportunity to kiss her. Besides the fact that he still didn't know how she would taste, she was accusing him of pitching for a different team.

If he hadn't so adamantly and, let's face it, obnoxiously, told her on the very first day they met that he wouldn't sleep with her, he would gladly show her how much he liked women in general.

And her in particular.

Jack had barricaded himself in the office all day and actually got some decent pages written. Although he wasn't ready yet to admit that his editor had been right to send Erin, the chip on his shoulder was wobbling.

He glanced at his dog, sitting in the bed and looking long-suffering and loyal. "Walk?"

Instantly the animal hopped up and eagerly trotted to

the door, waiting patiently for Jack to save the work and shut down the computer. He turned the knob and let the dog precede him outside and down the stairs. A view of towering mountains and pristine blue lake was, literally, a sight for sore eyes. And the fresh air felt great.

He jogged down the path after Harley and saw Brewster Smith outside the marina store. The sixtyish man had a full head of silver hair and a beard to match. Come to think of it, he'd be perfect for a mall Santa. Jack normally walked by but today he stopped.

He stepped onto the wooden walkway and under the awning over the store's entrance. The older man was moving racks of sale clothing and summer clearance merchandise back inside. "How's it going, Brew?"

"Good." Blue eyes assessed him. "You're looking better."

Jack wanted to ask better than what, but wasn't sure he'd like the answer. Then curiosity got the best of him. "Better than what?"

"Before Erin showed up."

"I have to admit I had a productive day. It feels pretty good."

"A fruitful day's work is good for the soul," the man said. "And that cute little writing coach you got there doesn't hurt, either. She's a piece of work."

"You'll get no argument from me." Jack wondered how the other man knew that she was a piece of work. "Does she come down here?"

"Every day," Brew confirmed. "Darn near talks my ear off."

"That sounds like her."

"But it's worth it because she makes the best buttermilk spice muffins I ever tasted." The other man pointed at him. "And if you tell my wife I said that I'll deny it."

"I won't breathe a word of it." But Jack felt the same way about her cooking. Her muffins were really good. "And you're right. Erin Riley can be a challenge."

The older man's silver eyebrows drew together as he scratched his beard. "What's wrong with her?"

"I'm not used to having anyone around. Being alone is more my thing."

"That so," Brew said.

"It works for me."

"Whatever blows your skirt off. But for now you should enjoy that little firecracker." The older man smiled. "And she's cooking up something special for tonight. If I wasn't taking the missus out to dinner, I'd have finagled an invite."

Jack heard "something special" and got an instant image of Erin after her workout then wondered if she would be wearing those skintight pants tonight. And just like that he was in a hurry to get Harley's walk over with.

"Later, Brew. Have a good evening."

"You do the same."

Jack whistled and Harley came running back from wherever he'd disappeared to and the two of them walked the path by the lake. As the sun dropped farther behind the mountain the chill in the air took a firm hold. Labor Day was over and Halloween was just around the corner. Before long it would be winter. Some people dreaded the isolation but he wasn't one of them. He was okay with his own company.

In spite of that he found himself rushing the dog through their routine, working him a little harder until Harley plopped at Jack's feet to be carried home. Jack complied and picked up his pace back to the house, then set the dog down at the foot of the steps leading up to the porch.

Jack stood there for a few moments, looking at the lights

glowing in the window. Someone was waiting for him. The realization stirred memories, not all of them good. Once upon a time he'd expected and anticipated a greeting after working all day but that dream had bitten him in the ass. Military training taught him a man didn't stay alive by making the same mistake twice. You might get lucky the first time, but your survival odds went down by a lot after that. In personal relationships, he hadn't even survived the first time.

Now that his head was on straight, he walked up the steps and in the front door. The fantastic smell of cooking food coming from *his* kitchen made his mouth water. Harley just trotted straight to where it was coming from and checked out what was going on.

Jack followed and his gaze was drawn to Erin, who was bending over to check something in the oven. She wasn't wearing the yoga pants, but her snug jeans were a close second in the framing-an-outstanding-ass department.

She looked at Harley, who stopped beside her. "Hello there, handsome. Be careful. This is hot."

Yes, it was, Jack thought, and he didn't mean the oven.

"He knows," Jack told her. "Animal instinct."

Stay away from anything hot because it's going to hurt. Good advice. Jack made note of that just in case his own instincts needed the reminder.

She closed the oven door and straightened. "Hi."

"Brew said you were cooking up something special tonight."

"Did that blabbermouth spoil my surprise?" She planted her hands on her hips and gave him a faux stern look.

"Hey, don't give me the stink eye. I didn't reveal any top secrets." He couldn't think of a single time that anyone had ever tried to surprise him. That gave him a weird feeling in his gut. "And, no, he didn't tell me what you're cooking if that's what you're asking. But it smells awful darn good."

"Fried chicken. Macaroni and cheese. From scratch, mind you. Not out of a box. Green beans. Biscuits, also from scratch. Pure comfort food."

"Why? Do you need cheering up?"

"No, but I thought it would be good for you. Your editor said there's more to a writer than typing words into a computer. Cheryl was adamant that it wasn't just your creativity that needed cultivation. It's about mind, body and spirit." She shrugged. "Makes sense if you think about it. How can your brain work efficiently if it's not fueled properly?"

If she'd done all this cooking for his body, Jack couldn't wait to see what she had planned for his spirit. There were a lot of things he could think of that had nothing to do with food.

He had to get his mind off how she looked in those tight pants and on to something more unexciting. "There's fuel and then there's fuel. I've had MREs that kept your body going. Basic. But this is carb-heavy."

"It's good for the imagination," she said.

The hell with imagination and creativity for crying out loud. He could think of some other parts of him that hadn't had any attention in a very long time. But before he could figure out how to verbalize a segue to that, or even how bad an idea it was to go there, the stove timer started signaling something.

"Mac and cheese is done." Erin smiled brightly and grabbed some heavy-duty oven mitts, then pulled a big, oblong glass dish out of the oven. She set it on a hot tray to keep it warm. "Dinner is officially ready. Have a seat and I'll set everything on the table."

Jack did as ordered, but damned if he didn't get the

strangest feeling. Not woo-woo, déjà vu weird, but regret. After marrying Karen this was how he'd pictured their life when he was finished with deployments for good. He'd go to work and when he got home she'd be cooking dinner. Mouth-watering smells would be coming from the kitchen. They'd have a little wine, some conversation about their respective days. He'd help her with the dishes, then make love to her. Eventually have kids. It would be everything he'd never had and always wanted. What happened was the exact opposite of that and taught him life was a whole lot harder if you had dreams.

"Are you okay, Jack?" She stood staring at him with the mitts still on her hands.

"Why?"

"You have the oddest look on your face."

"I'm good." He'd believed those memories had no power over him anymore but obviously he was wrong. Something about Erin had stirred them up. Forewarned is forearmed and he shook them off. "What can I do to help?"

"You can open that bottle of wine if you want some."

"I'll open it for you, but I'm more of a beer guy."

"Okay. Then you can handle beverages. I'd love a glass of chardonnay."

"On it."

Jack did as requested and set a wineglass in front of her and got a longneck bottle for himself. In the middle of the table was a platter of golden fried chicken, macaroni and cheese still bubbling and slightly brown on top, green beans and a cloth-lined basket filled with fluffy, flaky buttermilk biscuits. "This looks good."

"Sit down and dig in before it gets cold," she advised.

He'd never been quite so happy to follow an order and filled his plate. The chicken was crisp on the outside, tender and juicy in the middle. The mac and cheese was creamy and cheesy and a party in his mouth. And the biscuits? Holy mother of God—don't even get him started on the awesome, warm wonderfulness.

And that's when Jack had an epiphany. He had an attitude and was aware of it. He took great pride in his attitude, nurtured and cultivated being aloof and sometimes abrasive if necessary. Or, as he liked to think of it, succinct. But his attitude just couldn't stand up in the face of this feast.

"Erin, this is really good."

She smiled and the pleasure of his compliment glowed in her eyes. "I'm glad you like it."

"This is pretty much the perfect meal in my opinion."

"I thought it might be." She took a sip of wine.

"Why?"

"Well, who doesn't like fried chicken or macaroni and cheese?"

"Please tell me this isn't about that stupid saying—the way to a man's heart is through his stomach."

"Oh, please, Jack. We both know you don't have a heart." She laughed. "This is about how hard you've been working. Night and day as far as I can tell. I just wanted to make you something good."

"Mission accomplished. And you really nailed the menu." He took another golden brown chicken leg from the platter and bit into it, barely holding back a groan of pleasure.

"I'm no stranger to cooking for a man and tackling his taste buds." She forked up a bite of green beans.

"Your fiancé?"

"Yeah." The glow in her eyes slipped some. "He battled cancer and had chemo and radiation. His appetite dropped off to almost nothing and he was a big guy. He needed calories in order to fight the disease and it didn't matter whether or not they were the healthiest. Kale smoothies or chicken and dumplings. Which would tempt you more?"

"The second one. Hands down."

"The sicker he got, the harder it was to get him to eat. Toward the end it took what felt like hours to get a meal into him."

"Sounds like it was a tough time."

"Yeah." Then her perky hat fell off and she sighed. The sound was full of all the sadness and heartbreak she obviously had inside.

Again Jack kicked himself for throwing sarcasm at her personal life that first day she'd shown up on his doorstep. "How long was he sick?"

"Three years."

"A long time. And he proposed before the diagnosis?"

"Yeah."

"But you never married."

She pushed macaroni around her plate without looking at him. "There was a lot going on and the time never seemed right."

Jack had proposed to Karen just before he left for his first deployment because there was an instinctive need to be connected to someone and something from home. It wasn't a completely rational thing and was more about spirituality and not being alone. A man got pretty damn spiritual when he was facing the possibility of dying. And with her guy it was more than a possibility. He knew his shelf life had an expiration date.

"But he wanted to get married." It wasn't a question and a shadow slipped into her eyes. "He got weaker and weaker. Couldn't manage to do that."

He, not we, Jack thought. There was something she was keeping to herself and that seemed out of character for her. Something she was holding back.

But still, he couldn't help admiring her loyalty, which was more than he could say about his ex. She'd walked out and flatly refused to even try working on the marriage. Erin had never taken the in-sickness-and-in-health-till-death-do-us-part vow, but had lived it anyway.

He respected her for that, along with her determination. Unless she decided to direct it at him. She deserved someone as good at thinking about someone besides himself as she was.

Jack wasn't that guy.

Chapter Six

"How are you coming with those research topics?"

Erin was almost getting used to Jack Garner syndrome, which was what she called the way her heart skipped when he walked into a room. She had her computer set up on the kitchen table and looked away from the screen when he got her attention. Although, technically he'd gotten her attention when he appeared in the doorway looking very Jack-like. Which was to say that his animal magnetism was on full display. But he'd asked a question and it required a response, even a sarcastic one. Sarcasm was the only place where she could hide.

"Research? Really?" She leaned back in the chair. "You're suddenly in a hurry because you can't write the next scene in the book without knowing the mating habits of the blue-footed booby?"

"Fascinating creatures." His lips twitched.

"You're not fooling anyone."

Harley padded into the room and looked expectantly at Jack. He looked at the dog, then her. "I'm not trying to."

"Right." And she was the Duchess of Doubtville. "This research is nothing more than a distraction to keep me from bugging you."

"I think of it more as a flanking maneuver."

"Ah." She nodded. "An end run around your editor. Battle of wills. Cut off your nose to spite your face."

"You said it, not me."

"Very mature."

"Let's just call it my process." He leaned a broad shoulder against the doorjamb, folded his arms over his chest and grinned.

Erin's mouth went dry. She'd been there for over a week and thought she'd seen the best that Jack could throw at her. But she'd been so wrong. His scowl brimmed with sex appeal but the oh-so-masculine and tempting smile on his face right now could flat out make a woman's clothes come off.

Insert change of topic here. "Speaking of your process… How did the pages go today?"

"Oh, you know—" He lifted one of those swoonworthy shoulders in a shrug.

"Actually I don't. That's why I asked." The brooding look was back and that made her nervous—on a number of levels. But she focused on work. "Please tell me there are pages."

"Okay. There are pages."

His tone was flat with shades of mocking and she didn't know whether or not to believe him. "Let me look at them."

"They're not prime-time ready." He reached down to rub Harley's head when the dog put a paw on his leg.

"I'm not asking for Pulitzer Prize quality," she said.

"Just let me take a quick look. Make sure the story starts off with a bang—"

"No one gets shot in the first paragraph."

"Don't be so literal. That's not what I meant."

"I know what you meant." He moved farther into the kitchen. "But I'd rather talk about you."

"What about me?" she asked warily.

"Your loyalty. It's admirable."

This was about Garret and she didn't want to discuss anything more about her fiancé. She'd said enough last night. Apparently comfort food loosened her tongue. She'd danced around why there'd been no marriage and the truth was that he'd wanted it very much. Erin was the one who'd found excuses not to take the step. It was inherently dishonest not to have explained to the man she'd agreed to marry why she couldn't go through with it. And that wasn't admirable.

"I have a better idea," she said. "It's after two. I have no idea what you've been doing all day but this is the first time I've seen you. That equals hard work as far as I'm concerned. And you need a break. Let's go into town for groceries."

His blue eyes narrowed like lasers on her. "Now who's employing a flanking maneuver?"

She decided to take a page from his book, so to speak, and ignore that question. "Do you remember what I said about filling up the creative well?"

"Yes, but—"

"Keeping yourself isolated isn't the best way to cultivate inspiration. Besides, we're almost out of coffee."

"Uh-oh. Threat level goes to DEFCON five." But the expression on his face said the diversion hadn't worked and he wasn't quite finished with her yet. "I'd like to know more about the kind of man you accepted a proposal from."

This guy was mission-oriented and he had his sights set on her. But she just might have the mother of all flanking maneuvers. "Harley. Walk?"

The animal barked and started dancing around Jack. He ran to the door and back yipping excitedly. Jack met her gaze and saluted. "Well played."

It was her turn to grin and she didn't even care that he had her number.

A half hour later, after walking the dog, he drove the jeep up Main Street in Blackwater Lake. It was rush hour, if you could call it that here in this small but growing town. Chalk up the traffic to people from businesses along the main drag getting off work. For Erin the slow pace was an opportunity to check out Jack's stomping grounds a little more thoroughly.

They passed the Harvest Café with the adjacent ice-cream parlor beside Tanya's Treasures, the gift shop. Then there was the Grizzly Bear Diner, with its life-size statue of a ferocious-looking bear standing on rear legs with teeth bared and claws primed.

"I want to go to the diner sometime," she said. "Is the food good?"

"Never been there."

She couldn't believe that. "You've lived here how long?"

"A year and a half—give or take."

"And you have not once stepped foot in that restaurant?"

"No."

Erin waited but it seemed there wouldn't be an explanation coming anytime in the foreseeable future as to why so she took a shot in the dark. "Bar None is the extent of your social networking?"

"Didn't we already establish that loners tend to be alone?"

"Yes, but Jack—"

"What?"

"That's just so—" She struggled to come up with a word that wasn't quite so harsh, then decided what the heck? "It's so lonely."

"Not if that's what I want." He glanced over then, but the darn aviator sunglasses hid his expression. Apparently he saw something that deserved a comment. "And I order you not to feel sorry for me."

"That's just ridiculous," she scoffed. "You can't command someone how to feel."

"Has anyone ever told you that you'd make a terrible soldier?"

"Yes."

They were stopped at a red light and he gave her a long look. "Really?"

"No. I was just messing with you."

The corners of his mouth curved up. "That's what I thought."

Up ahead Erin saw a little storefront called the Photography Shop. In the window there were cardboard figures of an old west dance hall girl and a gambler with the faces cut out for tourists to pose for a picture. Behind that were what looked like framed photos of local scenery.

She pointed. "Stop there. I want to go in."

"You're messing with me again, right?"

"No. I want to look around."

"I don't."

"Then wait in the car with Harley." She glanced at the dog, who sat quietly in the rear seat. Then she looked at Jack and noted the muscle jerking in his jaw. "Or, you can throw caution to the wind and take a social field trip."

Erin really thought he was going to pay no attention to her request, but when the light turned green, he made a left turn and went around the block in order to pull up in front of the place. The lettering on the window said April Kennedy was the photographer. She remembered Sheriff Fletcher saying he was engaged to April and since his office was right across the street, she figured his fiancée owned this place.

She opened the car door and said, "I won't be long."

Just before she got out, Harley whined and she felt a little guilty about leaving him behind. The little guy didn't understand that his beloved human was calling the shots.

When she opened the shop's door an overhead bell tinkled and the two very attractive women inside looked at her. Both were in their twenties, one a strawberry blonde, the other a brunette.

"Hi. I'm Erin Riley."

"Jack Garner's research assistant." The brunette held out her hand. "April Kennedy."

The April who was engaged to the sheriff, which explained how she knew who Erin was. "Nice to meet you."

"Lucy Bishop." The other woman gave her a friendly smile. "Co-owner of the Harvest Café."

"I saw it. Looks like a nice place," Erin commented.

"It is. Lucy cooks all the food and it's really good," April said enthusiastically.

"I look forward to checking it out."

"So, is there something I can help you with?" April asked.

"I saw the photos in your window. Looks like scenes of the lake and mountains around here." Erin settled her purse strap more securely on her shoulder.

"They are."

She studied the breathtaking shots of twilight, when the mountains were backlit by the setting sun. And other scenes of the lake at different times of day. "Any for sale?"

"Not many," Lucy said, only a little rueful. "I've bought quite a few."

"My best customer."

"That will change once the walls in my new condo are decorated. Then you and Will need to be regulars at the café so I can pay for it all."

"Like we aren't in there all the time now," her friend scoffed.

That was probably where the sheriff had taken her after announcing to her and Jack at Bar None that he had a dinner date. "So you have a new condo?" she asked Lucy.

"Yes. Brand-new. Barely moved in. It's just at the foot of the mountains. Awesome views in the summer and winter."

"That's exciting."

"It is." But Lucy's attention shifted to the window that opened onto Main Street. "But maybe not as exciting as that dog."

Erin figured the animal's whining had gotten Jack out of the car. She glanced over her shoulder to confirm. "That's Harley. He's a Chinese crested."

"Is that Jack Garner with him?" April asked.

Erin smiled at the man standing guard over his pet. "Yes."

"I'd like to meet him," Lucy said.

"Me, too."

"He's a little shy. Be gentle with him."

The other two laughed, then April went behind the counter where the cash register was sitting and pulled out a camera. "I have to take some pictures of that dog."

Erin and Lucy followed the photographer outside, where she was introducing herself to a wary Jack. He was giving her camera the death glare.

"Do you mind if I take some pictures of your dog? He's

quite unusual. And I promise to make copies and give you some." April gave him a hopeful look.

He thought for a moment then said, "Okay."

She held up the camera and Harley froze as if he was posing. He even moved his head a little to the left and right as she snapped away. Then he turned sideways, as if for a profile picture.

"He's a natural." Erin laughed. "Jack, you should get him an agent."

"He's very unusual," Lucy said.

"Yes, but he grows on you," Erin told her. She looked at Jack, who was still watchful and alert. On guard. "I've heard that dog owners take on characteristics of their pets."

April studied him as if trying to confirm the truth of the words. "Would that be a good thing?"

Jack shrugged. "Harley is a better man than me."

The two women laughed but Erin got the feeling he wasn't entirely joking.

"So, how do you like Blackwater Lake?" Lucy asked him.

"Nice place."

"Didn't you buy Jill Stone's property on Blackwater Lake Marina?"

"Yes."

"It's beautiful out there. Quiet. Good spot for a writer," Lucy said.

The guarded expression on Jack's face told her it was time to change the subject. "This town is really different for me. I'm from Phoenix."

"I've been there," Lucy said. "I liked it a lot."

"Thanks for not making a crack about the dry heat."

"She's a little touchy about that." Jack almost smiled and gave her a look. He seemed to relax a little now that the focus had shifted away from him.

She could take one for the team. This couldn't have gone better. They had dragged him into a conversation but he was still socializing. She liked being a bridge.

"Well," Lucy said, "I managed to sneak away after the lunch crowd cleared out, but it's time to get back to the café for the dinner rush. Nice to meet you, Erin. And Jack, I hope you'll come by and check out the food at my place."

"Never know," he said.

"I really liked your book. I'm sure the next one will be even better than the first. I can hardly wait until it comes out."

"Don't hold your breath." Without another word he turned his back and got in the car.

Erin couldn't help feeling that the bridge she'd patted herself on the back for building moments ago had just collapsed on her head.

"Okay, so you've had a good brood. Now it's time to stop sulking and get it off your chest."

Jack turned off the jeep's ignition after pulling the vehicle to a stop at the house. They'd barely spoken while grocery shopping and neither of them had said anything on the drive back from town. Now the first words out of her mouth were that he was in a mood?

He released his seat belt and glared at her. "What happened to you supporting me?"

"That's what I'm doing." She wasn't the least bit intimidated by his look.

"If this is being supportive, I think I'll take my chances solo."

She took off her seat belt and angled her legs toward him. "Do you want to talk about what happened back there and why it made you crawl back into your man cave?"

For purposes of this conversation it would help him out

a lot if she didn't smell so damn good. Like flowers and sunshine. And look at him being all poetic. That proved his point. He couldn't think straight when her particular brand of soft skin and spirited push-back was so close he could grab her up and kiss her.

"I have no idea what you're talking about."

"I mean the way you went all strong, silent type on poor Lucy Bishop. She's obviously a supporter and the last time I checked, the goal was to sell books. It's hard to do that when you alienate your fan base."

"She started it."

Erin actually laughed. "You acted like a petulant little boy."

Probably some truth to that. He didn't much care right at this moment. "She said my next book is going to suck."

He expected a rapid-fire return from the copilot's seat and it was a couple of beats before reality sank in that he wasn't going to get one. He looked over and found her staring at him. "What?"

"I was warned that you would be difficult."

"Good to know I lived up to advance billing." That remark might have come from his inner, petulant little boy.

"But," Erin continued, "no one told me you were a diva."

Jack wasn't entirely sure about the definition of a diva, but thought it might involve outrageous demands for white-rose-petal-covered sofas and organic water from Bora Bora. That's not what this was about.

"It was the subtext of what she said," he argued.

"You know they say if you give twelve writers the same idea you'll get twelve completely different stories."

"What in God's name is your point?" he asked.

"You and I heard the same words and came up with two opposite interpretations. I believe she paid you a compliment, and is genuinely looking forward to reading your next book. You heard her say that you're going to fall on your face."

Harley jumped on the console between them and started to whine sympathetically. Almost as if the dog sensed Jack's inner turmoil. Erin didn't come right out and say it, but she was probably thinking that he projected his internal conflict by twisting innocent words. Could be some truth to that. And it made him a whiny toad, which was a rung or two lower than a son of a bitch.

"Understood." He looked at her and the sweetness in her face did not bring out the best in him. It made him want to push back harder. "Next time you decide social networking is just the thing, do me a favor."

"What?"

"Don't."

"But, Jack—" She looked down for a moment. "Creativity needs to be fed, watered and cultivated."

"I'm not a plant."

"I'm aware. It's a metaphor. You might have heard of them." She sighed, as if pulling her tattered patience together. "What I'm trying to say is that everyone needs contact with others."

"There's a reason I prefer being alone."

"And what is that?"

"People."

"You don't like people?" she asked.

"Roger that."

"So you don't trust anyone?" There was something awfully darn close to pity in those green eyes of hers.

"My army buddies. They're like my brothers. Closer. They had my back and I had theirs. I'd have taken a bullet for any one of them and they would have done the same for me." He met her gaze to make sure she was getting this.

"If any one of them needed help, I'd drop everything and be there to do whatever I could for them."

"And they would do the same for you." Her voice was hardly more than a whisper and it wasn't a question.

"Damn straight." Harley put a paw on his arm as if he understood all about duty, honor and loyalty. Jack almost smiled. "So, yeah, there are people I trust."

"But only a select few. No one else. And I'm pretty sure I fall into the no-one-else group."

"You said it." Even as the words came out of his mouth he realized she didn't deserve that.

"Okay." She nodded for a moment. "But here's something to think about, Jack. Trust happens for a lot of reasons. One of them is going into combat situations and finding out who you can count on." There was a lot less sunshine in her eyes when her gaze met his. "I suppose you could say life is combat. And telling someone only what they want to hear isn't the best way to have their back. If someone isn't afraid to lay the bad stuff on you, it's a pretty good bet that when they tell you something good, you can believe it's the truth."

Damn it, why did she have to make sense? He just wanted to be ticked off and he wanted to do it alone. She would call it crawling back into his man cave and frankly, hoo yah to that. It had been a bad idea to let her talk him into going to town and it was a bad idea to sit here now and listen to her being rational. And she smelled so good he wanted to bury himself in her.

He opened his door. "Harley. Walk."

The little guy let out an excited yip and jumped into Jack's lap then out of the car. He raced toward the marina. Without looking back at Erin, Jack followed after his dog.

Brewster Smith was breaking down today's sale display setup just outside the store. There were a few summer things left but the rest was fishing stuff. And it was getting pretty close to quitting time for the older man.

There was a chill in the air that had a lot to do with summer being over, but Jack also felt it inside himself. Probably it had been there for a lot of years, but he hadn't noticed until Erin's warmth showed him the difference.

Brew smiled when the dog bounded up the wooden steps and stopped beside him. He rubbed the animal's out-of-proportion head. "Hello there, Mr. Harley. You're looking fine today."

"Hey," Jack greeted him.

The older man gave him an assessing look, not unlike a military inspection searching for any breakdown in discipline. "Afternoon. You are not looking as fine as your dog."

Everyone was a critic. "Thank you."

"In fact," the man went on, clearly not getting that "thank you" meant don't go there, "you look like something's eating at you."

"Thank you again."

Brew nodded, indicating he got the message this time. "How are things?"

"What is it with everyone wanting to talk about the damn book?"

"Well, now, I can't speak for everyone. And I can't say I'm not curious about how it's coming along, what with your research assistant giving you a hand. But I sure did like the first one." Brew rubbed a hand over his beard. "That said, I wasn't askin' about the book so much as that pretty lady who's stayin' there with you."

"Oh." Jack was just about ready to admit the pretty lady stayin' with him had a point about him hearing something innocent that his subconscious turned into a negative. His only comment was "Erin is many things."

"I'd put talker at the top of the list." Brew laughed. "That little thing could babble the ears off a bull elephant."

The imagery made Jack laugh. Mostly because it was true. She turned out to be nothing like he'd first thought when she'd turned up here. The small, eager-to-please woman he'd believed he could torment into leaving had turned out to have a steely, stubborn streak. If anything she was the one pushing him around. How else did he explain getting him to go to town? And she spoke her mind whether he liked what she had to say or not.

Mostly he didn't *dis*like it.

"You're right about that, Brew. She's perky."

"A firecracker, that one."

Jack wondered if those washed-out blue eyes studying him so closely could see inside, what he was thinking. He sure hoped not.

"So that dinner she made the other night was pretty special," the old guy said.

"You mean the chicken, and mac and cheese?"

"That's the one. She brought some leftovers down to me for lunch the next day."

Because sweet and thoughtful was how she rolled.

"Yeah," he admitted. "It was good."

Brew nodded sagely. "Careful with that one, Jack. You know what they say about the way to a man's heart being through his stomach."

"I do. And no worries. Erin already told me I don't have a heart."

For some reason Brewster thought that was hilarious and laughed until Jack was afraid he would choke. He didn't think it was funny at all. And he had a sneaking suspicion that shrewd Brewster Smith was sending his own message. Jack figured his take on her was need-to-know and no one needed to know that she'd gotten his juices flowing, none of the ones that had anything to do with the creative process.

Jack had been between a rock and a hard place before, but this was different. Putting a move on her was pretty damn tempting, but he'd told her the very first time he laid eyes on her that they wouldn't be sleeping together. Besides not looking like a hypocritical ass, it would be dishonorable to compromise an employee. He was a lot of things—whiny toad and son of a bitch immediately came to mind—but a jerk who would put her in that kind of position wasn't one of them.

The burning question, and he did mean burning, was how the hell was he going to keep from being that jerk?

Chapter Seven

Erin was fed up with Jack's silent treatment.

Oh, there had been grunts and grumbles, a shrug here and there, but none of that counted as actual communication. It had been going on for a couple of days now, since his snit following their visit to town. Afterward he'd practically barricaded himself in his office.

They had meals together but very little conversation. The daily status meetings he'd agreed to had been aborted but that was about to change. Because she was useless this way and she was going to make him talk to her or die trying.

She grabbed her file folders with the bogus research acquired from the ridiculous subject matter he'd assigned to her. One of the topics caught her eye and was particularly ironic considering the way he'd clammed up.

"Erotic talk, my ass," she mumbled.

It was getting close to dinnertime and no way was

she putting up with his stonewalling for even one more meal. She was going to do her job. If he didn't like it, he could fire her and explain to his editor why the book wasn't turned in. Erin walked out the front door onto the porch, then turned right and stomped up the stairs to his office. Taking a deep breath, she knocked on his door. He had never given her permission to enter so, as usual, she opened the door and stepped inside.

Jack was at his desk typing on the computer as if he hadn't heard her. She wasn't sure she'd ever seen him from this angle, working. He had a very sexy profile and that was not a comforting thought as she prepared to jump into this confrontation with both feet. But she had to take a stand. She refused to be ignored.

"Hi, Jack."

His fingers stilled over the keys and he looked at her. "Do you want something?"

So much, she thought. "We haven't had a status meeting for a couple of days. I wanted to see how the book is progressing."

"You mean the one that's going to be better than my first book?"

"Wow, there's not a lot of forgive-and-forget in you, is there?"

"No."

She stared at him, hoping he would expand his answer, possibly explain what it was about Lucy's innocent remark that had hit a nerve. But he stared back and said nothing.

With a confidence she wasn't even close to feeling, Erin walked over to his desk and sat down in one of the chairs facing it. "How's the book going?"

"Fine."

"Great." That was a lie and she knew it, but she smiled

anyway. That deepened the frown on his face. "I'd love to read what you have so far."

"That's not part of my process."

She was this close to telling him what he could do with his process. Just in time she stopped herself because she had an epiphany. He was doing his best to goad her into losing her temper. This was him reverting back to his behavior from the beginning, trying to get her to go away.

"It's not going to work, Jack. And I'm a little disappointed in you."

"Now what did I do?" The words were defiant, the tone bored, but it was all to cover the fact that she'd surprised him.

"I thought we were getting along swimmingly and now you're trying to get me to quit again. And I have to say the surly act isn't very original. You're a creative guy. Surely you can do better than this."

He swiveled his chair away from the computer monitor and gave her his full attention. "What are you talking about?"

"This disappearing act of yours. We agreed to touch base once a day and you've violated our truce."

"I saw you at breakfast."

"That's not what I mean and you know it. We had a routine and for some reason you've gone rogue."

His lips twitched. "Gone rogue?"

"You're doing things alone. Not playing well with others. Shutting me out."

"Not true."

"Oh, please. I dare you to tell me how I'm involved in the work."

"In case you've forgotten, I leave you a list of research topics every day."

There was an air of self-righteous superiority because

he thought he had her on a technicality. As if what he gave her to do was seriously a job and the material he had her look up was important to what he was supposed to be working on.

"Really, Jack? Medieval weapons. South American coups and the history of orchids? We both know it's a smokescreen, throwing me a bone to keep me out of your hair."

"That's harsh. Mac Daniels could be a key player in the disruption of a South American political power grab."

Erin got the feeling he was enjoying his own power grab just a little too much. He was holding all the cards and that wasn't okay with her anymore. In a physical contest he could take her down with both hands tied behind his back. The man had training. He knew three hundred ways to incapacitate an opponent with a Q-tip.

All she had was her wits. Charm and feminine attributes could be weapons, too, but she wasn't sure she had a sufficient amount of either.

"Name one topic you've ever given me to investigate that you actually plan to use in your story."

He leaned forward and rested his elbows on the desk. "What do you have there?"

"These?" She held up several folders. "It's everything that I've worked on since I got here."

"What's in the top one?"

She'd been around him long enough to know a bluff when she saw it. Jack couldn't remember what he'd had her looking in to. That's how important it was.

Erin opened the file folder. "How to tease, tempt and tantalize your lover with words."

"That was on the list?"

"Technically the focus of it was how to talk dirty. But I fine-tuned the theme."

"Ah." He nodded. "How about the next file?"

"Don't you want to know what I found out about this?" She pointed to the material that had put a hitch in her breathing and shot a look in his direction that dared him to hear her out.

"Sure. What have you got?"

"Okay. Let's start with the language of love." She felt a stab of satisfaction when the smirk on his face disappeared. "There's talking dirty, which is simply a graphic account of lust, and then there's listening to your lover express pleasure in how attractive, special or sexy you are."

"I can't see Mac doing either."

"You haven't heard everything yet." This was where she got even with him for all this research. "Moving on to voice. The tone you use with your partner can be more arousing than what you say. I found out there are exercises one can do to develop a richer, more pleasing pitch to make your voice sound naturally sexy. In my opinion the most effective ones are for the jaw, tongue and lips."

"Good to know, Erin. Great job. You are incredibly thorough—"

"I'm not finished." And speaking of jaws, the muscle in his was tight, as if he was gritting his teeth. *Take that, Mr. Action-Adventure.* "You're going to love this. I need to tell you about sexual communication during a first meeting." And the first one she'd had with him didn't count. The one where he'd flat out told her to not even think about sleeping together because that wasn't going to happen. "Some of this just might come in handy for Mac."

The amusement on his face was now missing in action. "He can handle himself just fine."

"Still, he might meet a gorgeous woman with the figure of a goddess and instead of complimenting a particularly well-endowed body part, it's more effective to express appreciation about a standout quality in a person."

"So instead of Mac saying to a woman 'you must work out a lot because your—'" he stopped for a second, let his gaze linger on her chest, then met her gaze "'—muscles are nicely developed,' he should compliment her persistence?"

"Exactly."

"Okay, Erin, you've made your point. Let's not—"

"I haven't gotten to the best part yet." She flipped through her notes and something caught her eye. "Let's talk fantasies."

"Let's not." His voice wasn't resonant or modulated. It was practically a growl and filled with warning.

"Just hear me out." In for a penny, in for a pound. She was poking the bear and couldn't seem to stop. He'd shut her out of the work. In her mind she had nothing left to lose. "Imagine a scene where Mac says to Bianca, 'I want to make love to every inch of your body. I want to discover your most secret fantasies, the part of your soul that you've never shared with anyone else before. Let your erotic imagination go wild—'"

Was it getting hot in here? Or was she heating up because his eyes were almost certainly focused on her mouth?

"Mission accomplished. Research rebellion understood."

The words were barely a whisper but Erin swore his breath caressed her naked skin. She felt tingles everywhere—there wasn't a place on her body that wasn't touched. Her heart started to pound and she was sure he could hear.

That was the problem with unintended consequences. This was supposed to get to him, but she'd turned herself on.

What was it they said about revenge being a double-edged sword?

Erotic talk was intended for your partner, which technically Jack wasn't. She couldn't swear to it, but his breathing seemed to be more uneven than when she'd started reading from her notes. That was just her own wishful thinking. It would be too humiliating if he saw that she had the hots for him. She needed to get out of here before this bad idea turned into a disaster.

"General rule of thumb, Jack. Don't punish your reader and put all the research into the book." They both knew he wouldn't use any of this. She leaned over and put her folders on the corner of his desk, then stood to make her escape. "I have to go."

She made it to the door before Jack reached her and she hadn't even heard him move.

He put a gentle hand on her arm. "Wait—"

Erin could feel him behind her—the heat and danger. His body barely touching hers. He didn't need to do any exercises to make his voice more appealing, at least not for her. The deep sound was soft, sexy and seductive. A single word had her hesitating.

"I need to go." She turned and caught her bottom lip between her teeth.

Jack's eyes darkened with intensity and he blew out a long breath. "When you do that— God, Erin—"

"What? I'm not—"

He touched his lips to hers and she realized this was the definition of irony. Half her mission was accomplished. He was using his mouth, all right, but not for talking.

One thing was clear—she hadn't gotten over the attraction she'd felt the first time she saw him. This man, this awesomely hot guy, was kissing *her*. Miss Nobody. The touch was soft and sweet, and suddenly getting enough air into her lungs was a challenge—in the best possible way. It was hard to think straight, but one thing she knew for sure—this extremely wonderful, mind-boggling moment could end in a heartbeat so she was going to enjoy the heck out of it while she could.

She pressed her body to his, stood on tiptoe and slid her arms around his neck. He groaned again against her mouth, but she could feel the vibration in his chest, which was pressed to hers. His fingers slid into her hair, cupping the back of her head, and he cradled her in a way that made her heart race.

With his arms wrapped around her he half lifted her and moved a step, backing her against the door. She could feel his muscular thighs, her breasts snuggled to his broad chest and—oh, God—how much he wanted her. *Her!*

She brushed her palm over his cheek and jaw, smiling at the way his stubble scraped her hand. "Jack—"

"No—" He braced a forearm on the door and studied her with dark, smoky eyes. His breathing was ragged and she sensed he was just barely holding on to his control. She slid her hand down his chest and to the belt of his jeans, tugging his T-shirt from the waistband.

He put a gentle hand over hers. "That's a dangerous game you're playing."

"What if I don't care and want to play anyway?"

"If you were smart you'd walk out that door."

"That was my plan." She could barely get the words out, what with having so much trouble breathing. "I'm not the one who prevented me from leaving."

"Yeah. About that—"

She touched a finger to his lips, stopping the words, and stared straight into the raging storm in his eyes. "Don't you dare say it was a mistake. I don't want to be some-one's blunder."

"No. Not you." He hung his head for a moment, then his gaze blazed into hers. "It's me. I'm not a good risk. This isn't smart—"

"You're telling me the sensible thing is to stop this right now. And frankly that just made up my mind."

"Good. It would be best—"

"Stop right there." She jabbed her index finger into his chest. "I don't want to come to my senses. Just once I want to do something without planning it to death. No more making a decision because it looks good on paper. Live life to the fullest everyone says. Grab on with both hands and enjoy it. Without regrets."

Erin knew with every fiber of her being that if she walked away now she would deeply regret it forever. For a long moment Jack studied her and she felt as if she could reach out and touch the conflict churning through him. Finally he sighed, and she was almost sure he'd surrendered.

Jack took her hand and the lead, heading toward the doorway that led to the bedroom. Stopping by his desk, he opened the bottom drawer and pulled something out of a box. She caught a glimpse of a square packet and realized it was a condom. Thank goodness he'd been thinking because she was still in not-coming-to-her-senses mode, the one where rational thought wasn't allowed.

He tugged her down the hall into the bedroom where she'd spent her first night under his roof. It was dark outside now, but he didn't turn on the light. There was enough coming from the hall. As soon as they were through the doorway, he kissed her with a desperation that matched her own. With his mouth and hands on her, all she could think about was how good this felt.

He stopped long enough to drag his shirt off in one easy, quick movement and she tried to do the same with hers. But the material got hung up on her hair and Jack seemed eager to help her out, then tossed her shirt into a shadowy corner of the room. With the light to his back, she couldn't see his eyes when he cupped her breasts, but his hands were shaking slightly.

He brushed his thumbs over the tips of her plain white bra and she wished for an estrogen miracle that included pretty, feminine underwear. Kissing her neck and shoulder, he reached behind her and unhooked that plain white bra, letting it drop to the floor between them.

He straightened and settled his gaze on her, drawing in a quick breath. His voice was a little hoarse when he said, "Pretty."

Somehow lacy lingerie didn't seem quite so important all of a sudden. She rested her palms on his chest and wanted to say something, but she had no idea what. Instead, she just felt…the dusting of hair. The contour of muscle. The taut abdomen. It gave her a moment of pure clarity—the last one for a long time.

Lacy, matching bra and panties didn't make a woman feel feminine. What did that was the way a man touched her. A gentle, commanding caress that activated every nerve ending in her body and made her hormones snap to attention.

Slowly he backed her toward the bed and when she felt the mattress behind her legs, she kicked off her shoes and sat. He dropped to one knee and undid the button at the waist of her jeans. Without conscious thought, she lay back on the bed and let him draw the zipper down, then lifted her hips so he could slide off her pants.

A moment later he dragged off the rest of his clothes and slid in beside her, pulling her into his arms and kissing her into a frenzy of need.

His fingers traced the edge of her panties as he slipped his hand between her legs, not quite touching her where she most wanted to be touched. Then he hooked a thumb into the waistband and dragged them off. When he touched her where she wanted him to, she arched her hips and shamelessly pressed herself into his palm, where he cupped her.

His breathing grew increasingly harsh until finally he left her long enough to take the condom out of his jeans pocket. He put it on, then kneeled on the bed, gently nudging her legs apart before covering her naked body with his own. He took most of his weight on his forearms so as not to crush her. The warmth and sheer wonder of being skin-to-skin washed over her.

With one hand he brushed the hair away from her face. "You're looking at me like that."

Like she had the first time they'd met. And he was looking back, his eyes dark with heavy-lidded desire. No man had ever looked at her like that before. The realization shattered her control and she reached for him, arching her hips again, letting him know she wanted him.

He slid inside her slowly, deeply. It was a delicious sensation as she felt herself close around him. He rocked into her and she wrapped her legs around his waist, hanging on for dear life as she came apart in his arms.

He held her close as pleasure rolled through her, tremors in its wake. When they stopped, she pressed her mouth to his neck and nibbled kisses down his chest. With a groan from somewhere deep inside, he buried his face in her hair as he thrust one more time and followed her into release. She held him as he'd done for her and they stayed locked in each other's arms for a long time. Frankly, Erin didn't ever want to move, but that wasn't an option when her stomach growled. It was dinnertime.

Jack smiled tenderly. "Someone needs to be fed."

"Something tells me I'm not the only one."

"I'm not saying you're right, but with my training I can get by longer on less."

"Nuts, berries and bugs?"

"If necessary," he agreed, his lips twitching.

"Gosh darn, we're fresh out of survival provisions."

"Bummer."

"What about steak, baked potato and salad? If it would make you feel better I can lie and tell you I picked the greens in the forest."

His stomach rumbled right on cue. "As you might imagine, I don't much care where the greens came from."

"Okay. Then you have to let me up."

"Roger that." Surely there was reluctance in his eyes.

Before she could decide whether or not it was real or imagined, he rolled away and grabbed his clothes off the floor before leaving her alone. The sound of the bathroom door down the hall was her cue to get up and she dressed as quickly as possible.

A few minutes later they were both back in his living room/office. Erin noticed that the bottom drawer of his desk wasn't all the way closed. She glanced at Jack and saw that he'd been looking in the same place. After her remark about survival rations she must have provisions on the brain because she couldn't resist asking. "Office supplies?"

"There's a legend in the writing world that a well-stocked office makes one a better writer." He lifted one broad shoulder in a shrug.

She'd seen that shoulder without a shirt and the simple, masculine gesture was now a major turn-on. That was her signal to leave. "I'll go get dinner started."

"Okay. Meet you downstairs."

She nodded and walked out the door. If she didn't miss her guess, he had no desire to talk about what just happened. That worked for her. The problem with coming to your senses was the return of rational thought.

On the first day they'd met Jack had said in no uncertain terms that he was never going to take her to bed. Erin didn't know whether or not to be pleased that she'd made a liar out of him. Or completely shocked that she'd crossed a professional line. When his editor had hired her to look after him mind and body, she probably hadn't meant for Erin to sleep with him.

She had a strong work ethic so that made her feel bad enough. Even worse was the guilt she felt toward the man she'd agreed to marry, then didn't before he died. Sex with Jack Garner was the best she'd ever had.

And she had no idea where things went from here.

Chapter Eight

The next morning, Jack stepped out of the shower, grabbed a towel from the bar beside it and dried off. It was an ordinary start to the day—or it would be if he hadn't slept with his research assistant the night before. The same assistant he'd once asked whether or not she'd ever slept with a man. Now he knew for a fact she had, because he'd been there.

That was bad enough, but the part that made him feel as if he was living in an alternate universe was where she hadn't talked about it. During dinner she didn't bring it up even once.

He'd waited, alert and ready, and had been braced for anything. Had an apology all rehearsed in his head. Along with a promise that it wouldn't happen again. It was no lie that he was a bad risk. He had the juvenile record and bad marriage to prove it. Erin was the kind of woman you protected so she could find the guy who deserved her and would make her happy.

Jack wasn't that guy.

The thing that messed with his head was that she acted as if it never happened. Or in any way let on that she had regrets or felt used. But now she'd had a whole night to think things over. This morning at breakfast she was going to hit him with the rocket-propelled grenade of what happens now.

After shaving, combing his hair and putting on the usual jeans and T-shirt, he took one last look in the mirror. "I'm ready for you, little Miss Sweetness and Light."

Jack opened his bedroom door and was immediately hit by some mouth-watering smell coming from the kitchen. Coffee mixed with sausages and potatoes. He was hungry and knew it was probably too much to hope she would wait until after he ate to launch her verbal offensive.

Following the smell of food, he walked down the hall to the kitchen. As usual Erin was there and the coffee had been brewed.

She had her back to him and was whipping something in a bowl with a wicked-looking metal thing. Probably she was pretending that stuff being worked over was his face.

Jack braced himself and tried to put on his not-a-care-in-the-world hat. "Morning."

Her body jerked and she glanced over her shoulder. "Good grief, you startled me. I didn't hear you. But I guess when you're army Special Forces, you get pretty good at sneaking up on people. Obviously your training stuck because I had no idea you were there."

"Understood." He was trying to decide if her cheerfulness was forced and she was prattling more than usual. It was hard to tell.

"I'm making omelets today. And there's sausage." Apparently Harley was helping by standing guard at her side.

"Sounds good." Jack studied her eyes, which were bright green and so clear and beautiful it was hard to look away.

His gut told him she didn't have a deceptive bone in her body and if there were any hard feelings the evidence would be right in front of him. His assessment was a complete blank on negative feelings, which should have been a relief, but wasn't. That didn't mean she wasn't planning a discussion over breakfast. Best keep up his guard and repeat that apology one more time in his head.

"Do you want coffee?" she asked.

"Does Harley like walks?" He laughed when the little dog yipped and scurried over to him, doing his level best to follow orders and not whine. Jack squatted and scratched the hairless body. "Sorry, buddy. Didn't mean to say the *w* word. It's going to have to wait. I have a scheduled meeting this morning."

Erin poured the beaten eggs into the hot pan, then glanced over her shoulder and smiled. "Nine o'clock sharp."

His comment wasn't about time confirmation as much as giving her an opening for that discussion. She'd been locked and loaded when she came upstairs to reestablish a perimeter around the status meeting she'd insisted on having, then proceeded to bust his chops about the research he'd given her. After that...

He was so turned on.

And that's where military training had deserted him. You couldn't always be in command of a hotspot, but you learned discipline over your own actions at all times. Last night this woman took him down without firing a shot. Thus the need to establish rules of engagement—if she brought up the subject.

While she stood watch over the cooking eggs, he poured

coffee into the mug she'd set out for him. His favorite mug, he noted. The one that read, Go Big or Go Home.

"Can I help?" he asked.

"Yeah. Make toast. The bread's already in, just push it down."

"Roger that." He did as requested and buttered the slices when they were ready.

A few minutes later they were seated at the table across from each other, just like every morning since she'd arrived on his doorstep. His plate was loaded with a spinach-and-cheese omelet, fried potatoes, sausage links and toast. Hers looked the same but with significantly smaller portions. She dug into the food like someone who'd been marooned on an island for weeks. Was it his imagination, or could she be avoiding conversation?

She chewed a bite of toast and swallowed. "So, I'm curious."

Okay, not avoiding talk. Here it comes, he thought. "About what?"

"How did you happen to choose a dog like Harley?" She speared a potato with her fork. "Not that he isn't a sweetheart. But, let's be honest here, he's not really your type."

Did he have a type? If they were talking women, the one across from him was the polar opposite of the kind he usually favored. The looser their standards, the better he liked them. With Erin, her standards had standards. But she'd asked about Harley. And he was so relieved that she hadn't brought up close encounters of the sexual kind that he didn't even consider not answering.

"I saw Harley when I walked by an animal shelter in California. He was standing at attention in the window and wearing a camouflage T-shirt. He was, hands down, the least appealing animal in the place. Pretty much the ugliest dog I'd ever seen in my life."

"So why did you take him?" She cut off a bite of egg and put it in her mouth.

"I didn't. Not then, at least."

Erin stopped chewing for a moment and stared at him. She swallowed quickly, then said, "So you went back for him? On purpose?"

"I went back," he said, "but not for him. My mission was to talk myself out of any imaginary attachment. My fall-back position if that didn't happen was any dog but him."

"A more handsome one who would complement you?" One of her delicate eyebrows lifted, daring him to contradict her.

He wished he could, especially because there was a flattering subtext in the question. She apparently thought he wasn't so bad to look at. Jack wasn't particularly vain, but hell, how did he fight that?

"I was sure one of those other dogs would grow on me," he admitted.

"But that didn't happen and you took him home," she persisted.

"Nope. Not that day, either."

She set down her fork. "So, what happened? Obviously this story has a happy ending because he's here. Did he escape from the shelter and stow away in your car?"

"I think he would have if he had opposable thumbs and was tall enough to reach the door handle." He laughed at the image. "No. Third time was the charm."

"Ah, so he wasn't an impulse buy. The acquisition was premeditated."

Jack didn't have a snappy comeback to that so he was honest. "There was something about him. Every time I saw him he stood proud and dignified. Like a good soldier who was presenting himself for inspection to a superior officer. The next thing I knew, I had a dog."

"Oh, Jack—" She smiled. "That's a great story."

He looked at her, waiting for a zinger to follow the praise, but those eyes of hers went all soft and gooey, as if he was some kind of hero.

That wasn't good.

The dog had plopped himself beside her and she reached down to rub his head. "You chose wisely."

"You were not one of his groupies the first time you saw him," he reminded her.

"I was hasty. He's a keeper."

"You think?" Jack honestly wanted her opinion.

"I do. He's proof of all those sayings. Beauty is only skin deep. It's in the eye of the beholder. Don't judge a book by its cover."

"Yeah," he said dryly. "That."

"This little guy has grown on me," she admitted.

"I think the feeling is mutual." And there was a lot of that going around, Jack thought. Because she was growing on *him*.

That was the only explanation for why he'd compromised his principles and slept with her when he'd sworn it would never happen. He'd told her that to her face before asking if she'd ever been with a man. He'd tried his damnedest to ignore her and she'd destroyed his willpower with her erotic talk.

"Thank you for telling me that, Jack." She had that mushy hero thing going on again.

"No big deal."

"That's where you're wrong. I think opening up about something so personal means you're starting to trust me." And she looked ridiculously happy about it.

Suddenly things had gotten even more complicated than a simple clarification of where they stood after sex. Erin was the kind of woman who wanted promises, the white picket fence, a family. She'd been engaged, for God's sake. But Jack knew that a promise wasn't worth the powder it would take to blow it to hell. As much as he wished it could be different, there would not be a repeat of last night.

No discussion necessary.

He was counting on the discipline he'd learned in the army to keep him from disobeying his own direct order.

Jack had apparently received her message loud and clear about the folly of assigning her absurd research topics because today's list *could* be relevant to an action-adventure story. Erin had compiled some information on search-and-rescue, bullying and drug-sniffing dogs. But her favorite, by far, was diamonds. As in fencing stolen ones.

She looked at the pictures on her computer and sighed. "Definitely a girl's best friend. Men can break your heart, but a diamond will never let you down."

"Should I be worried that you're talking to yourself?"

Erin jumped, then saw Jack in the doorway. "I wish you'd stop doing that!"

"What? Worry?"

"No." She pressed a hand to her chest, over her pounding heart. At least she told herself it was pounding because he'd startled her. It was probably something more serious than that but she wasn't going there. "Quit sneaking up on me. Wear a bell or something. I'm not a covert op that requires stealth protocols."

"Someone is crabby."

"Someone was just dandy until you scared the stuffing out of her."

"Understood."

The word was crisply spoken, all military discipline, but the grin was a targeted weapon that did nothing to return her heartbeat to normal and everything to rev it up again. Darn him. It was like some kind of mind control. If he grinned and ordered her to take off her clothes, she'd be naked in a hot minute. But that was just wishful thinking. Going to bed with him again was like eating a whole bag of potato chips in one sitting. Giving in to temptation might be satisfying in the moment, but the process of getting rid of the negative consequences would be long and ugly.

On the other hand, maintaining the status quo was practical.

She knew it was late afternoon but not what the time was. Diamonds tended to make a girl lose track of everything. The sun getting lower in the sky said it was inching toward the dinner hour, which meant she should cook soon.

"Why are you here?" she asked.

"It's my house?"

"What I meant to say was, are you finished working?" she asked.

One dark eyebrow rose and he leaned a broad shoulder against the wall. "Are you?"

She was going to lob that ball back in his court. "I could be. Or not. Because I'm not the one who's at the beck and call of my process to write a book."

"I see." He nodded thoughtfully. "Well, let me put it this way. My process is getting cabin fever."

"So you're finished working?" she persisted. "I need a simple, direct answer."

"Yes. I'm going into town," he added.

Erin was almost sure they'd had a conversation about filling up the creative well, an idea he'd mocked. She couldn't resist rubbing it in a little. "That will be good for your process. Have fun."

"You're going with me."

"Oh, you don't want me." She was sure about that. He'd never said a word about them sleeping together, which told her how much she mattered. That slipup was a one-time thing. "I'm quite certain they keep your chair warm at Bar None. There's probably a sign on it. You should go make another new acquaintance."

"It's not Bar None I have in mind."

"Grizzly Bear Diner, then." She nodded. "Looks like a fun place. You should check it out."

"Another time." He straightened away from the wall and there was something in his eyes that was almost vulnerable. "I'm going to the Harvest Café."

"Wow." A vivid image of his last encounter with the café's co-owner was still fresh in her mind. "Are you going to talk books with Lucy Bishop?"

"Actually it's her partner, Maggie Potter, I want to see. And this is long overdue."

Erin tried to be on her toes with him at all times, but that one she really hadn't seen coming. "Why?"

"I could tell you, but..."

"You'd have to kill me," she said wryly.

"You're very dramatic."

That was ironic coming from the man who went all wonky and weird at the mention of his second book, or she should say work-in-progress. At least she hoped there was forward momentum. But she decided to take the high road and not point out that he was the pot calling the kettle black.

"Okay, then. When do you want to leave?" she asked.

"Now."

"What about Harley?" Come to think of it she hadn't seen the little guy all afternoon.

"I think the health department frowns on animals in restaurants."

"Smart-ass." She shook her head. "I meant, he'll need to be fed."

"Already done. He had a walk and is in my office. Probably sound asleep after exercise and wolfing down his dinner."

She couldn't come up with any other excuse. "I'll go get a sweater."

When the sun went down it was pretty dark and isolated out here by the lake. Besides the lighting down at the marina, the one on the front porch was all that cut the shadows. As they walked down the front steps together and headed for the jeep, Erin fought the feeling of intimacy the twilight created. This wasn't a date. It was her job.

She wondered if this was how Stockholm Syndrome worked. Forced confinement created feelings you wouldn't ordinarily feel for the person you were cooped up with. Yeah, that's all it was.

She climbed in to the passenger seat at the same time Jack slid behind the wheel. A shiver went through her and she wouldn't let it be about anything personal.

"It's getting cold," she said.

He turned on the car and instantly headlights sliced into the night. "That happens in Montana when it gets to be October."

"Halloween is just around the corner. Before you know it the holidays will be here."

"So? It's the same as any other time of year. Except colder."

"How can you say that? Everything is decorated. There are parties. And presents." She sighed. "Family."

"Yeah, that's my point."

She could see his rugged profile in the glow of the dashboard lights. He didn't look happy. "You don't have family?"

"Didn't say that."

"So you do have relatives."

"Singular," he explained. "Mom."

Erin remembered him saying his dad had disappeared. "Where does she live? Around here? Do you see her often?"

"Don't see her. That's the way she wants it."

"You can't be serious."

"According to her, I was trouble from the moment I was born. Didn't sleep much, got into everything, then I turned into a teenager and the trouble I got into was the against-the-law kind."

"You were arrested?"

He nodded. "Fell in with a bad crowd. Always looking for the next kick and got caught breaking and entering."

"What happened?"

"I was almost eighteen and still a juvenile. Lucked out with a sympathetic judge, who figured this was my first offense and I might benefit from structure and discipline."

"Since you joined the army, I'm guessing you took his advice."

"No one was more surprised than me at how well the life fit. I even went the extra mile and joined the army Special Forces, Ranger Battalion." The words were positive but there was a raw note in his voice. "The downside is we train for action, but when we're sent in bad things happen to good people. There's a price to pay."

"Yin and yang."

"What?" He glanced at her.

"Up and down. Ebb and flow. Good and bad. It's the balance of life." She tried to keep her voice light, but wondered why he was suddenly telling so much about himself. "You just go with it."

"As easy as that?" he asked.

"Didn't say it was easy. That's just the way it is and you make the best of it."

"Doesn't anything get you down?" He started to say more, then stopped. "I mean, obviously losing your fiancé was rough. I don't mean that. But you're always so damn...perky."

"I don't always feel that way." Things with her fiancé weren't what she'd let Jack believe. She would always regret that her feelings changed, but there was nothing she could do to alter his terminal diagnosis. She'd put on a happy face and done her best to keep him from knowing the truth before he died. "I just make an effort to be cheerful."

"You set a high bar."

"It's not about being an example to anyone else. I don't judge."

Jack didn't say anything for the rest of the drive to Blackwater Lake. He drove into town and found a parking place on the street, right in front of the Harvest Café. After exiting the car they walked inside and stopped by a glass-front bakery case. There was a sign that read, Please Wait to be Seated.

They weren't there more than a minute when Lucy Bishop approached them. The expression in her blue eyes could best be described as wary. "Welcome to the Harvest Café. Table for two?"

"Yes," Jack said. "Nice place you have here."

"Thank you. Right this way."

Erin glanced at Jack, a look that said the woman's polite yet cool tone was his fault, but she wasn't sure the message had been received. They followed her to a table in the back corner, a little secluded and a lot intimate. There was a high shelf containing country knickknacks, including a copper pitcher and metal washboard. The tablecloths were shades of gold, green and rust. Coordinating cloth napkins had eating utensils wrapped up in them and were on every empty table.

"Here you are." When they sat across from each other she handed each of them a menu. "I'll be your server tonight."

"I thought you were the chef." Jack's voice was disarmingly friendly. "And, by the way, something smells fantastic. I'll take one of everything."

"I appreciate that." Lucy smiled, revealing a dimple in her left cheek.

"Obviously I can't sample everything. So, what do you recommend?" The man had his charm set on stun. That was as close to an apology as he would go.

"I've heard from more than one person tonight that the meat loaf is particularly good. And we have carrot-ginger soup that's pretty yummy if I do say so myself. But only if your taste runs to that sort of thing."

"I'll keep that in mind," he said. "But I have to ask. You're the chef, so why aren't you in the kitchen?"

"I'm wearing both hats right now. My partner, Maggie, is having dinner with her fiancé." Lucy nodded toward a young couple sitting two tables away. She was beautiful, he was handsome and they couldn't take their eyes off each other. "He's Sloan Holden. A real estate developer. In fact his company built the condo complex where I bought a place."

"I see." He looked over then fixed his gaze on Lucy. "There's no rush, but when she finishes dinner, would you ask her to come over? I'd like to speak to her for a moment."

"Anything in particular?" Lucy's wariness had disappeared but she looked puzzled. "Since you haven't eaten yet, it can't be a complaint about the food. And I've been incredibly gracious so it can't be about poor customer service."

"It's all good." Jack smiled, but it disappeared when he glanced at Maggie. "I knew her husband."

"I see." Lucy's eyes widened just a little. "I'll let her know."

Erin watched her walk over to the table where Maggie and Sloan were having an after-dinner cup of coffee. The dark-haired woman listened, then looked surprised as she glanced at Jack. She said something to the man with her, then stood and came over.

"Hi. I'm Maggie. You're Jack Garner."

"I am." He stood to shake her hand. "And this is Erin Riley, my research assistant.

"Nice to meet you," Erin said.

"Same here." Then Maggie looked at Jack. "Lucy said you knew my husband, Danny?"

"Yes, ma'am. I served with him in Afghanistan. I just wanted you to know that I'm very sorry for your loss. He was a good man."

"Yes, he was."

"All Danny talked about was you and his baby on the way."

Maggie smiled a little sadly. "That sounds like him."

"He also said that Blackwater Lake was the best place in the world. That's the reason I checked it out when I was looking for property to buy."

"How do you like it so far?" the other woman asked.

His gaze slid to Erin for a fraction of a second before he answered, "It's growing on me."

"If he were here, he would be the best tour guide to make sure you saw all our little town's charms." A wistful expression slid into Maggie's eyes. "I'll always regret that our daughter will never know her father."

Jack looked down for a moment, then met her gaze. "I would be happy, if you'd like, to share my memories of Danny with her."

"She's two and a half." Maggie smiled. "But it would mean so much if you could do that when she's old enough to understand."

"It would be an honor."

"Thank you, Jack."

Erin was a sucker for emotional moments and this one got to her big-time. Crusty loner Jack Garner had volunteered to do a nice thing for a fallen brother's little girl. Tears gathered in her eyes and it took all she had to keep them there.

How was a girl supposed to resist him?

Where was a bag of potato chips when you really needed to eat your feelings?

Chapter Nine

Several days after Jack's meeting with his friend's widow, Erin was still regretting passing on that bag of chips in the grocery store. She was confused and uneasy in equal parts.

Confused because she'd been almost sure he meant *her* when he'd said the town of Blackwater Lake was growing on him. But his behavior toward her hadn't changed. If anything he'd become more distant. He was still man-caving in his office and avoiding her as much as possible.

A better book coach would be happy he was writing, and she was. Except that she hadn't seen any pages and he might be working too much. Again last night she'd heard him upstairs during the night. When she passed his room this morning on her way to the kitchen, his bedroom door was open and he was nowhere to be seen. Like the last couple of nights he'd probably slept in the room off his office, the one where he'd made love to her.

No. Not love.

It was just sex. Really good sex, but nothing more than a physical release for both of them. If she repeated that enough, the message might actually become true. She hoped so because she'd never been the type to get intimate with a man just because he was pretty to look at.

While making coffee, she heard the front door open and close, then Jack appeared in the kitchen. He filled a glass from the water dispenser on the refrigerator and started to guzzle.

When he took a breath she said, "Good morning."

His only response was a nod. He'd been for a run already. The shorts and sneakers were a clue. But the deciding factor was his black T-shirt with bold white letters saying ARMY on the front. It was sweaty and clung to his upper body in a very intriguing way. She remembered how good it felt when they were skin-to-skin… And this was a train of thought that needed to go off the rails.

"So, you've been out for a run bright and early."

"Yeah." He finished the rest of the water. "Clears my head."

"Did your head need clearing?" If so, she thought, what had to go?

"Figure of speech."

"Oh. I just wondered. Because you were in your office during the wee hours last night."

"Are you stalking me?" There was amusement in his eyes.

"Only if stalking is defined by hearing you pace at one in the morning."

"Didn't mean to disturb you."

"You didn't." Liar, liar, pants on fire. And the disturbance had nothing to do with being awake. She'd never gone to sleep and he was the reason she couldn't. "So you were working on the book that late?"

"Yeah." But his gaze didn't quite meet hers.

"Be careful, Jack."

"Of work? I thought that's what you wanted."

"Yes. In balance."

"Inspiration and balance aren't always compatible," he said.

"That's a fair point. But burnout isn't the goal." And speaking of burnout, he was looking so hot she might just go up in flames. "You barricaded yourself upstairs all day, barely taking time to eat. Then you put in more time during the night. It's not healthy."

He thought about that for a moment. "Did you mother-hen Corinne Carlisle?"

"I didn't have to. She didn't work day and night, then go running to clear her head."

"Maybe she should."

"She's over sixty."

"Spring chicken. Jogging shakes things loose."

"If you knew Corinne, you'd know that her idea of shaking things loose is a gin and tonic when happy hour rolls around."

"High five, Corinne." There was a gleam in his eyes when he said, "So she took care of the spirits. Your job was body and mind. How did that go?"

"Good—healthy food for the body and talking about her book kept the work fresh in her mind. Speaking of the book—"

"I'm going to take a shower." Abruptly he turned and walked out of the room.

So much for meeting the enemy head-on. There was mischief afoot.

She thought about what he'd said and on the surface it seemed as if he was engaged. But something was off. He was vague, deflecting the questions. Wry, coy, sarcastic and mocking. Similar to the way he'd acted when she first arrived and he'd tried to intimidate her into going away. Before he'd admitted he had no book.

She was into him now and not just because she'd been hired to be. No question he wasn't an easy man, but there was more to him than that. He had a soft spot for a homely dog and came to Blackwater Lake because a fallen brother had told him it was the best place in the world. He'd offered to tell a little girl about the father she would never know.

Erin wanted to help because she'd chipped away at his hard shell and underneath it discovered there was a man she genuinely cared about. They said the way to a man's heart was through his stomach and she was going to find out whether or not that was true.

Ten minutes later Jack walked back into the kitchen and poured himself a mug of coffee. It was annoying and unfair how fast the man could clean up and look as if he'd been through hair and makeup on a movie set to get ready for his close-up. Of course, the not shaving saved time and made him look like the guy most likely to have women falling at his feet.

"What's for breakfast?" He sipped coffee and met her gaze over the rim.

She poured a beaten mixture into the heated pan on the stove. "Scrambled eggs. Sausage. Biscuits and gravy. And blueberries. I hope you're not disappointed."

"Are you kidding?"

"I never joke about breakfast. It's the most important meal of the day."

"Of course, it needs to be sampled first. But judging by the smell, it will beat army chow for sure."

"If I wasn't here," she said, sneaking a look at him while stirring the eggs, "what would you be eating?"

"Coffee. Something out of a can."

"Seriously? That's sad."

"But true," he said.

"What you need is a cooking coach. So you can feed yourself when I'm gone."

His expression didn't change but there was something smoky in his voice when he said, "Did Corinne survive on her own?"

"Yes."

He shrugged as if to say "okay, then." "I'm starving."

"You're in luck."

"Because I'm starving?" One dark eyebrow rose.

"No. Breakfast is ready."

The table was already set and she put the food on it. Jack sat across from her and filled his plate, then wolfed down what seemed to her enough to feed an army. And it hadn't come out of a can. A girl could only hope it was appreciated.

She deliberately channeled conversation to the weather or topics equally innocuous because they were due to meet in half an hour. The questions would keep until then.

When he was finished, Jack actually thanked her for cooking, which kind of left her speechless. Then he refilled his coffee and went upstairs to his office. She did the dishes and cleaned up the kitchen while mentally preparing for the coming conflict. In the last couple of days she'd felt more like a housekeeper than anything else. She'd given him the latitude he'd asked for, but it was time to do what she'd been sent here to do.

One minute before nine o'clock she climbed the stairs and knocked on his office door, then let herself in. "Hi."

He looked up from his computer monitor and frowned. "What are you doing here?"

"Status meeting. Remember?"

"We already had the update. Before breakfast."

"Not even close." She sat on a chair in front of his desk. "That was about the hours you're putting in. I'd really like to see what all that effort has produced."

"You don't trust me?"

"With my life? Absolutely," she said with complete conviction. Meeting his gaze she added, "But you are an expert at evasive maneuvers and I don't have faith that you'll be straightforward now."

"I'm hurt."

"Oh, please. This is me." She was prepared to die on this hill and refused to be intimidated by the glare he shot at her.

"You want to see pages."

"Give the man a gold star." No matter how much she wanted to, she refused to look away.

Apparently he got her take-no-prisoners message because he reached down to open a desk drawer. He pulled out pages, but after glancing at them, he had an odd look on his face then quickly shoved them back. He retrieved another stack of paper from another drawer and held it up. "See? Pages."

When he made a move to put them away she said, "Not so fast."

"What? You see them."

"Very funny. What are you? Fourteen? And trying to pull a fast one because you didn't do your homework? This isn't my first rodeo."

"Do you have any idea how much I hate it that you're a teacher?"

"It's a dirty job but someone has to do it." She sighed. "I'm on your side, Jack. I just want to read what you've got so far."

He didn't hand over the pages, just put them on the desk

in front of him. "I'm asking you to wait until the book is finished."

"I get it, Jack. I understand that every writer has a process and this is yours. But I find myself caught in the middle. Your editor is entitled to reassurance."

"I know. Just tell her I'm putting in so many hours you're concerned for my mental health."

She couldn't help smiling. "Because she'll find that so encouraging?"

"Why not?" There was no surrender in this man. Bravado and bluff was how he rolled.

"She's going to want something tangible. Or at least to know that I've seen hard copy. It's not unreasonable."

"Negative."

Erin wasn't sure if that was a no or an assessment of the request she'd just made. "This isn't negotiable."

"They need polishing."

"Do we need to have the diva conversation again?" She was only half teasing. "Please, Jack. My job is on the line. It's what I was sent here to do."

He looked at her and with every second that passed his eyes grew darker, more defiant. Just when it seemed he was going to refuse, he flipped through the stack of paper and handed it over. When she took the pages their hands brushed and she felt the touch all the way to her toes. That had never happened when she'd coached Corinne.

"Thank you." For the pages or the thrill? She wasn't sure.

"Don't say I didn't warn you."

It seemed she got a warning about him every day, for all the good it had done. But that wasn't what he meant. "I'm sure they're really good."

"I hope you're not disappointed."

He meant his work but she took it a step further. Every

day that went by upped the chances that she was going to experience a deep feeling of disappointment when this assignment ended. Jack wasn't someone who would be easy to forget.

Erin couldn't get downstairs fast enough to read the pages and it left her wanting more, which was the opposite of disappointed. The chapters were really good. Mac Daniels met a mysterious woman with brown, highlighted hair and green eyes. He called her Little Miss Perky and she wasn't extraordinarily beautiful, like his ex-wife. But she was vulnerable, yet strong. A compelling combination. And she talked a lot.

She thought that sounded a lot like her, which was part of the reason she wanted more. And the writing was sharp, intense, like Jack. The good news was he had pages— strong pages. The bad news? He hadn't given her any research topics. It was possible he didn't need any information for the book or was dropping the ridiculous pretense. Either way he was working and that had been her job. Speaking of which, she needed to update his editor.

After making sure about the time in New York, Erin called the publishing house and hoped to get Cheryl's voice mail in order to minimize details. But no such luck.

"This is Cheryl."

"Hi. It's Erin Riley." She paced the kitchen.

"Hey. I was just thinking about you. How are you holding up?"

Interesting way of asking about her well-being. Not "how are you," but "how are you holding up?" "I'm fine."

"Is Jack behaving himself?"

The better question was whether or not Erin was. And the answer would be no. She'd practically seduced him. But that was one of those pesky details better kept to herself. She decided to fall back on the Jack Garner conversational method of evasive maneuvering.

"That's why I'm calling, Cheryl."

"Oh, God, you're quitting. He's so difficult you can't take it anymore."

He was certainly difficult, but leaving had never occurred to her. At least not before her assignment was completed. "He's a complicated man."

There was a moment of silence on the other end of the line. "Does that mean you're not quitting?"

"It means I wanted to let you know he's moving forward on the book."

"That's fantastic. Have you read it?" Relief and excitement mixed together in the other woman's voice.

"I have. It's very good."

"Great news," Cheryl said. "I want to get it in the publishing schedule but I need an idea of time frame."

"He's touchy." Considering Erin had called him a diva that was extraordinarily diplomatic.

"That's not news, Erin. It's the reason you were sent there. How close to finishing is he?"

That was a very good question. It presupposed Erin was in control of the situation. That so wasn't the case. How to not lie and cover for both Jack and herself. "I believe he's seeing the light at the end of the tunnel."

"Can you get him to commit to a completion date?"

Jack didn't seem the committing sort, but that observation was strictly personal. Her best guess was that it wasn't wise to put pressure on him just yet.

"He's clicking along and I'm reluctant to say anything that might get in the way of his progress."

"Okay. I'll hold off on that for a little bit. Obviously you have a handle on the situation since he hasn't sent you packing."

Not for lack of trying. At first what kept her there was the prospect of more assignments and travel. Now she was staying for the man. God help her.

"He wasn't warm and fuzzy when I showed up, but I've seen a lot of layers to him." Naked didn't count.

"Okay, then. I trust your instincts."

She wasn't so sure that was prudent. "I'll do my best."

"Just keep doing what you're doing," Cheryl said. "I've got another call and need to take it. We'll talk next week?"

"Sure. Bye."

Erin clicked off and the best she could say about the conversation was that she still had a job. Even though it didn't feel that way because she didn't have anything to do.

This might be a good time to stock up on office supplies. Based on Jack's modus operandi the last couple of days, he'd be locked in his office indefinitely and wouldn't know whether she was around or not. But she left a note next to her laptop on the kitchen table in case he came looking for her. Then she grabbed her purse along with the keys to her rental car and headed out for the town of Blackwater Lake.

During one of their trips to town, Jack had driven by Office Supplies and More, which was on Blue Sky Street, just off Main. She parked in the lot and entered through the back door. The baskets—hand held and rolling—were kept up front by the cash register. She walked past the counter where a cute, petite teenage girl was standing.

"Welcome to Office Supplies and More," she said automatically.

"Thanks," Erin replied just as automatically.

"Can I help you find something?"

She scanned the aisles and noted that there were signs clearly identifying where things were located. Pens and pencils. File folders. Notes. Calendars. There was nothing exotic on her list so this should be easy. "I'm just going to browse."

"If you can't find something, just let me know."

"Will do."

Erin picked a rolling basket, which would hold more, then decided to go from one end of the store to the other. Step by step and logical, the complete opposite of the way things had gone for her from the moment she'd met Jack Garner.

"Never too late to turn things around," she muttered to herself.

From what she'd observed of his office, Jack did a lot of his writing on legal pads, probably blocking out a scene in longhand while his subconscious churned on ahead and ideas came flooding in. She put a box of mechanical pencils in the basket.

On the paper aisle she found a giant economy package of yellow legal pads and grabbed it. Sticky notes in different sizes and colors were next to go in. Those were all over the place on his desk.

And in the bottom drawer he kept condoms. Probably not purchased from the office supply store. The memory of being with him put a hitch in her breathing and regret in her heart. Everything had changed after sex. He'd opened up about Harley and there was that "aww" moment with his army buddy's widow. Since then he'd been avoiding her as if she had cooties. She even missed obnoxious, abrasive Jack and that was pretty pathetic.

After adding highlighters and file folders to her basket she wheeled it to the check out counter, where a pretty, blue-eyed blonde just beat her in line.

"Hi, Miss Fletcher—" The teenager stopped and shook her head. "I'm sorry. Mrs. Miller."

"Don't worry about it, Glenna. I'm still not used to the married name."

Maybe it was loneliness, but Erin couldn't resist. She asked, "How long has it been? Since you were married, I mean."

"Seven weeks." She smiled dreamily, then looked more closely. "We haven't met. My first name is Kim."

"I'm Erin Riley. Are you any relation to Sheriff Fletcher?"

"He's my brother."

"And more," Glenna chimed in. "He was the man of honor at her wedding."

"Like a maid of honor, only a guy," Kim added.

"I met him at Bar None. Big guy. Major hunk factor. I'm trying to picture him in a bridesmaid's dress and just not loving it."

"He agreed to the job and was absolutely the best. But he drew the line at a dress or carrying flowers." Kim laughed. "Will mentioned meeting you at Bar None with Jack Garner. You're his research assistant."

Sort of. Her job description was kind of fluid at the moment. "I work with Jack."

"Talk about hunk factor—" Kim blew out a long breath. "I've seen him a couple times at Bar None. He's Heathcliff and Mr. Darcy rolled into one."

"If you're saying he's a brooding loner, you would be absolutely correct."

"Sorry. That was my inner literature geek talking. I teach honors English at Blackwater Lake High School."

"So do I. I mean the teacher part. I'm a substitute in Phoenix. My current assignment is temporary." Saying it out loud stopped her cold. The idea of leaving was remarkably unappealing. It's not the way she'd felt when her time with Corinne Carlisle was up.

"Mrs. Miller is the best English teacher I ever had," Glenna interjected. "All the kids want to be in her class."

"I love my job and that helps. I enjoy working with kids, although it's not for the faint of heart. But you know that."

"I do."

"Is that why you're moonlighting? Working for a famous author?"

Erin smiled. Jack was many things but definitely not for the faint of heart any more than teaching. "I just love the written word. The way each one is put together in dialogue and paragraphs to tell a story. And Jack is very good at what he does."

Kim's expression turned thoughtful. "I've got some kids in my honors class who are natural storytellers. They might get some valuable information from Jack Garner. And even for the students who aren't great writers it might spark an interest in reading. It's hard to get across to them how important it is, so anything out of the ordinary might jumpstart them. Do you think he might be interested in talking to the kids about what he does?"

"I can ask."

"That would be so awesome," Glenna said.

"What have I told you about the word *awesome*?" Kim's expression was teasing.

"It's overused. Exercise your brain and come up with something more creative," the teen said, obviously parroting what was preached in class.

"Exactly." The teacher beamed. "But it would be pretty awesome if he would say yes."

Erin didn't want to burst her bubble, but the odds of being struck by lightning were probably better than convincing Jack to give a motivational talk to high school kids.

"I'll mention it to him," she agreed. "But you may have

noticed. He's not particularly social. Please, don't get your hopes up about him."

The words were barely out of her mouth when Erin realized that same warning could apply to her. She was teetering on the edge of having feelings for Jack and somewhere deep inside she wanted him to return them.

She really should heed her own advice and not get her hopes up about that ever happening.

Chapter Ten

Jack was standing outside the marina store with Brewster Smith when he saw the rental car return. Erin got out and something inside him relaxed. He'd come downstairs expecting to see her and found the note she left. It crossed his mind that he'd pushed back a little too hard on her reading the chapters and she'd had enough. Left before he'd learned to cook for himself. That reminder about her being gone soon had struck a nerve.

She glanced in their direction and waved, then set a couple of bags on the front porch before walking down the slight hill to join them. Harley ran ahead to meet her and she dropped to one knee and enthusiastically rubbed him all over.

Jack wouldn't mind if she greeted him that way and his body tightened at the thought of having her in his arms and getting her naked.

Not necessarily in that order.

But there was one problem with the scenario. Another intimate encounter would be like walking into an enemy ambush without body armor or a weapon. That's why he was maintaining a safe zone. Although keeping it up was taking a toll.

She gave Harley one more rub, then stood and walked over to them. "Hi."

"I see you made it to town and back," Jack said.

"Did you get my note?"

"Yes." For some reason it wasn't especially reassuring.

"Then what's the problem?" she asked.

"You were gone for a while" was the best he could come up with.

"Did I make it home before curfew?" She lifted one eyebrow before smiling brightly at the older man. "How are you, Brewster?"

"Fit as a fiddle. Yourself?"

"Fine. How is Mrs. Smith's cold?"

"Stubborn. Like her." He lifted one shoulder in a shrug. "But better. Although she still has a pretty bad cough."

"I'm sorry to hear that. Has she gone back to work yet?"

Brewster shook his head. "Someone is covering for her at the thrift store. She's getting impatient, though."

"That's a good sign. I wish I could do something to help. Maybe a batch of chicken soup?"

"Lucy Bishop already brought some over." His blue eyes twinkled. "But Aggie wouldn't mind some of your macaroni and cheese."

"I don't believe she's ever had it." Erin laughed. "But I'll whip some up for you to take home to her."

"If it's no trouble."

"Not at all. It's easy."

Jack watched her relate to the older man with a potent combination of friendliness and charm. She made it look effortless, natural. Dangerous to him. She'd been in town about two hours and he'd noticed. The house had never felt empty before. Not until her. That was too damn close to missing her.

"So you went to town?" Brew asked.

"Yes. All the stores are decorated for Halloween. Pumpkins, ghosts, skeletons. Spiderwebs up in the windows. It's so cute. I bet Christmas is really something here."

The old man nodded. "We're all about holidays in Blackwater Lake. In fact there's a big costume party at the community center for Halloween."

"Do you and Mrs. Smith go?"

"Wouldn't miss it." He looked at her, then Jack. "You coming?"

"I don't know." She looked as if she wanted to.

"Worried about a costume?"

"Maybe," she admitted.

"Thrift store. Good place to get ideas." Brew nodded then glanced up at the house. "So what's in those bags you brought back?"

"That's what I'd like to know," Jack said.

"Stuff to make you a better writer." She grinned wickedly.

He wondered if she'd read the chapters yet and found what she thought about his writing really mattered to him. "What's wrong with my work?"

"Not a thing," she assured him. "Love the beginning, by the way."

Did she really? Or was she just being nice in front of Brewster? Give him body armor and a tactical mission and he was secure and confident. But coughing his guts onto a page? The doubt made him feel like a teenage boy afraid to ask a girl out on a date. Later he would grill Erin for her real opinion.

"So what did you get that's going to make me brilliant?"

"Sticky notes. Index cards. Pencils. Highlighters."

Brewster scratched his head. "That's just stuff."

"Writers love stuff," Erin explained. "It makes them feel empowered."

"That true?" the man asked him.

"Yes." Jack slid his fingertips into the pockets of his jeans.

"Seems to me ideas come from here." Brewster tapped a finger to his temple. "Taking your head out for a spin now and then couldn't hurt."

"He means filling up the creative well." Erin's tone clearly said "I told you so."

"I know what he means," Jack said.

"Talking to people is fun. You should try it sometime."

Apparently it was too much to hope her needling would be contained in front of the older man. "I have no beef with talking. It's people that are the problem."

She got a funny look on her face. "Have you ever talked to kids?"

"Not if I can help it."

"You offered to talk to Maggie's daughter about her dad," Erin pointed out.

"That's different."

In the waning daylight Jack studied her. Something was up. He knew her and this wasn't idle banter. There was something on her mind and he wasn't going to like it.

"What did you do?" he asked.

"Nothing." She folded her arms over her chest and met his gaze.

"Something's going on. You might as well come clean."

She stared at him for a few moments, then nodded. "It's Saturday in Blackwater Lake—"

"The edited version," he suggested.

"I ran into Kim Miller—"

"Who?"

"She's Sheriff Fletcher's sister. You remember him. Your friend from Bar None, the place where you take your inner writer out for a spin to make friends?"

"I know who he is. It's her I don't have a clue about."

"She teaches honors English at Blackwater Lake High School."

The dots were not yet connected but he had a bad feeling about this. "So you two bonded over teaching Shakespeare. I felt the ripple in the Force all the way out here."

She tilted her head and gave him a you're-going-to-the-principal's-office look. "Sarcasm is so unattractive. And you're going to feel really bad when I get to the good part."

"Regret is my middle name. Go for it."

"Kim is a fan of your work. And a teacher. A good one, according to Glenna."

"Who is Glenna?"

"She works at Office Supplies and More. And she's one of Kim's students."

"And what does her opinion have to do with anything?"

"She's a fan of Kim's. As a teacher myself I can tell you that a good educator never overlooks a teachable moment. She's hoping to highlight the importance of reading. And when you think about it, giving of your time is an investment in job security. You need readers to buy the books you write." Erin glanced at Brewster, who seemed to be enjoying this back-and-forth a lot. "Kim wants you to speak to her honors English class about what it's like to be a career writer."

Jack had his doubts about whether or not he had a career as a writer. He'd sucked at being a son and husband. Soldiering was the only thing he'd ever been good at. And his publisher had sent him a babysitter to get this book done.

How could he talk to kids when he didn't know what the hell he was doing?

"You shouldn't have promised," he told her.

"I didn't. Just said I would ask you."

"Mission accomplished and the answer is no."

"Why, Jack?"

He was an imposter? Had nothing to say to them? A guy like him was not a good role model for impressionable teens? *Pick one of them*, he thought. *Or all of the above.*

"How about I don't have time," he finally said.

"Baloney." She put her hands on her hips and might have been glaring at him. The sun had just disappeared behind the mountains throwing them into shadow so it was hard to tell. "It won't take more than forty-five minutes to an hour. You'd lose a couple of pages but those kids are giving up valuable instruction time. Because their teacher believes it's important. I do, too."

Damn it. Those words turned out to be heavy artillery because, for reasons unclear to him, he didn't want to disappoint her.

Maybe just one more try to back her off. "Now isn't a good time."

"You could live anywhere you want, but you settled in this town." Brewster didn't butt into a conversation unless he had something to say. Apparently he did now and it wasn't good. He wasn't smiling.

"That's just an address," he countered.

"Not in Blackwater Lake. If you're bleeding or on fire folks call 911. For anything else they pitch in when asked. They share what they've learned, what they know."

"What if they don't have anything to share?"

"You'd be surprised. Won't know unless you try," the old man said. "And you try because being neighborly is a way of life here. If you don't get involved, the magic of this place doesn't work."

Jack kept his mouth shut even though he wanted to ask, "What magic?" The grizzled, practical old guy talking about it at all was enough to get his attention. If he said no now it would look like he had a heart the size of a sunflower seed. He knew when he'd been outflanked. "Okay. I'll talk to them."

Erin smiled, a cheerful, satisfied smile. As if she'd known he would give in. "You won't regret it, Jack."

"I'm pretty sure that's not true." The look on her face irked him so he added, "I'll do it on one condition."

"Oh?"

"I'll talk to the class, but you're coming with me."

She saluted, being a complete smart-ass. "Yes, sir."

Her job was to take care of him—body, mind and spirit. His body was pretty happy what with being well fed and the spectacular sex. She'd managed to touch his mind, too, in ways she didn't even know. But he had his doubts about the spirit thing.

Still, he figured the job description included having his back while attempting to communicate with teenagers.

God help them.

And him.

Erin wouldn't exactly say Jack looked afraid to go into the high school classroom, but it was a good bet that facing heavily armed enemy combatants was a more comfortable fit. The two of them stood just outside Kim Miller's room while teenagers swarmed up and down the hall, hurrying to their last class of the day.

After Jack's less-than-enthusiastic agreement to show up, Erin had contacted the teacher and they'd agreed Friday would be best. With the weekend staring them in the face, the kids were restless anyway and they'd probably learn more from Jack. Judging by his dark and brooding expression, he didn't agree.

"Take a deep breath, Jack. The kids are going to love you."

"Why?" He shot her a don't-give-me-that-crap look. "It's too late for a personality transplant and no one has ever accused me of being charming or approachable."

"Doesn't mean you aren't."

"Seriously?"

"Never too late to turn over a new leaf." She met his gaze, trying to infuse him with some of her optimism. The dark look in his eyes didn't falter. "Come on. Embrace the moment. You're just here to talk to them."

"About what?"

"Didn't you prepare some notes?" Now she had a knot in her stomach.

"No."

Oh, boy. The hall was much less crowded now. In a few minutes there would be some kind of signal to let students know they'd better be in their seats. And Jack had nothing ready for the class he would face. She was his research assistant/book coach. This situation was the equivalent of thirty seconds left on the clock in a football game, just enough time for one or two plays to win the game. It came down to coaching and she had to give him something.

"Okay, this is basically the same principle as writing what you know."

He stared at her. "Not even close. Two different things."

"What I mean is, start out by telling them your personal story. You know yourself." Better than anyone, she thought. "Talk about you."

"That will take fifteen seconds."

"Oh, please." She rolled her eyes. This man was complicated. She could talk about him for hours. "Give them the high points. Maybe five minutes or so. Then open it up to questions."

"And if there aren't any?"

"You thank them for not hitting you with spitballs and we leave. It will give us more time to poke through the thrift store for Halloween costume ideas."

"What?"

"We're shopping."

"Torturing teens isn't enough? You want to torture me, too—"

A loud signal broadcast over the school's public address system interrupted his protest. "Saved by the bell," she said.

With the kids in their seats, Kim saw them in the doorway, smiled and motioned them to come in. "Class, I have a surprise for you. The test will be on Monday. Anyone who didn't study just got a reprieve." There was a collective sound of relief. "We have a guest speaker."

Erin nudged him farther into the room, where about twenty teens sat in several rows. The teacher's flat-top desk was in the front with the chalkboard behind her. They walked over and Erin introduced him to Kim.

"I'm a big fan," she said, gushing.

"Thanks."

In a low voice Erin said, "I'm going to sit in the back. You'll be great."

"I'll get even with you," he muttered.

She slipped quietly to a chair against the rear wall, trying not to be a distraction, but there was no worry about that. The guys stared at him in awe and the girls were smitten at first sight. It was like being in the same room with Indiana Jones.

"Everyone," Kim continued, "this is Jack Garner, author of the phenomenally successful book *High Value Target*.

Has anyone read it?" All but one or two hands went up and there was an enthusiastic murmuring as hero worship ratcheted up. "Good. I thought you all might enjoy hearing what Mr. Garner has to say. So, take it away, Jack."

"Thanks." As the teacher moved to the side, Jack stood alone.

He could have looked more uncomfortable, but Erin couldn't see how. Still, the students didn't know him like she did and wouldn't see it.

"Okay. Here's the deal. I figure you get lectured to enough." He glanced at Kim. "No offense, Mrs. Miller."

"None taken."

"So, I didn't prepare notes. I'm just going to tell you a little about myself then open this up to questions." He thought for a moment, then seemed to make a decision. "I was raised by a single mother and never knew my dad. Not a very good student. Didn't have a lot of options beyond high school so I joined the army. After leaving the service, I wrote *High Value Target* and you all know the rest."

He wasn't kidding about his life story taking five seconds. But that was such a skeletal description of him and Erin had been around teenagers long enough to know they wouldn't let him get away with not filling in some of the blanks. When he asked for questions, again nearly everyone in the room raised a hand.

Jack looked surprised, but relaxed a little. He pointed to a dark-haired girl in the front row. "Tell me your name, then ask your question. That goes for all of you."

"Mackenzy Bray," she said. "And this is my question. Mrs. Miller told us there are a lot of options for us when we graduate. I'm wondering why you picked the army."

"The choice was kind of made for me. It's true I was a bad student. But I left out the part about being arrested. Not proud of it and don't recommend the experience. Before you ask, it doesn't matter what I did. The important part is the judge went easy on me because I was just under eighteen and it was a first offense. He made it clear it better be the last and said I lacked structure and discipline. Strongly recommended joining the military in whatever branch would take me. That turned out to be the army."

"Did you like it?" A boy in front of Erin blurted out the question.

Jack grinned and you could almost hear every female heart skipping a beat. "Speaking of discipline and not following orders."

"Sorry." The kid's voice was sheepish. "My name is Blake Hoffman."

"And you want to know if I liked it since there was some arm-twisting to get me there." He nodded. "The answer is that no one was more surprised than me when I took to the life and was good at it."

A girl's hand went up and he pointed to her. Erin recognized the teenager from Office Supplies and More. "Glenna Smith, Mr. Garner—"

"Call me Jack."

"Jack," she said shyly. "The bio in your book said you joined Special Forces, Ranger Battalion."

"Yes. That's how much I liked the life. I wanted to be the best of the best and serve my country."

"So why retire from it?" she asked.

"Good question." There was a guarded look in his eyes. "I just knew it was time. Next question."

"Did you always want to be a writer? Russ Palmer," the boy added.

"No. In fact I wasn't much of a reader until I needed something to do during downtime. And there was a lot of it. A buddy gave me a book and I was hooked. Read everything I could get my hands on."

"Why did you start writing?" Kim shrugged. "You already know who I am and this is my classroom. Rank has its privileges."

He grinned, then half sat on a corner of her desk. "To be honest, along with the positive of joining up, the fact is soldiers train for war. There are some things no one can prepare you for. It leaves a mark. I started a journal and really liked putting words on paper. That evolved into a fictional character with a story." He shrugged. "Against all odds it was published."

"And a success," Kim said.

Erin saw a shadow cross his face and knew it was doubt, the intangible enemy dogging him now. The expression was completely opposite of the way he'd looked when talking about being a soldier. He'd once told her it was all he was good at, but she disagreed. And he couldn't see the way he was connecting with these kids. Until you'd stood in the front of a classroom and witnessed teenage eyes glazed over with boredom, you couldn't appreciate how involved these kids were now.

She was very surprised that he opened up to her about his rocky youth, but chalked that up to progress in their working relationship. Today he'd related some very personal and not very flattering details about himself to these kids—strangers—and it was a huge step for him. For them it was a lesson that there was no single path in life to success. Good information for them to have. He'd been honest about the bad stuff so his message had a profound impact.

"What's your next book about? Chloe Larson," she added.

Erin's stomach knotted again. The last female who mentioned his next book got the cold shoulder. He was touchy about the sequel and wouldn't discuss it. She held her breath, waiting for him to respond. Or walk away without another word as he'd done to Lucy Bishop.

He glanced at the class. "You might remember from the first book that Mac doesn't have a job. And he has a limited skill set. It's either law enforcement or private investigation."

"Which one does he pick?" the girl persisted.

"What do you think?" he asked.

She thought for a moment. "He liked the military, so I believe he'd become a cop."

"A case can be made for that," he said. "But Mac's going into the private sector. Too many rules in police work."

"There are a lot of similarities between you and Mac." That was from Glenna. "Do you break the rules, Jack?"

His gaze met Erin's over the heads of the kids and somehow she knew he was remembering the two of them ending up in bed with tangled legs and twisted sheets. Since they'd both ignored the implied guiding principles of a working relationship, that made them equally guilty of breaking the rules.

He smiled, a mysterious expression on his face. "Let's just say you have to know and understand the rules before breaking them."

"What does that mean—"

The bell sounded and the kids groaned. She caught murmurs of disappointment because some of them still had questions. That had the ring of success to Erin's way of thinking.

"Always leave them wanting more." Kim laughed. "I'm quite sure that's the first time any of us were sorry to hear the last bell on Friday afternoon. Class, let's give Jack a round of applause. If you're nice, maybe he'll come back and talk to us again."

"Count on it," Jack said.

The sound of hands clapping was instantaneous and enthusiastic. He lifted a hand to acknowledge them, then moved to the back of the classroom, where Erin stood waiting. After putting his hand at the small of her back, he quickly ushered her out the rear door before anyone could slow him down with another question.

"That went well," she said, trying to keep up with his long strides.

"Depends on what you mean by *well*."

"You really connected with them."

"That and a buck will get them a soda."

"You underestimate yourself, Jack." She glanced up at him, the tight mouth and tense jaw. "You have a lot of wisdom to pass on. It was enlightening for them to know that the choices they make have consequences—some good, some not."

"Yeah, I'm just a real role model."

"You're determined not to believe that so I'm not going to waste my breath. But I'll tell you this and I believe it with all my heart—books give you the power to reach people."

"Right."

"They picked up on the fact that Mac has a lot of you in him. Through your characters and the truth in your words, you can inspire anyone to do whatever they set their mind to."

His pace slowed and he dropped his hand. For a moment he met her gaze, then the corners of his mouth turned up. "Good try. But I'm still not ready to let you read everything I've got."

"I think what we have here is the lesser of two evils."

"What?"

"Reading your book or the thrift store."

"Never thought I'd say this without a gun to my head, but let's go shopping."

Chapter Eleven

"So, you've made up your mind about going to the community Halloween party." Jack glanced over at Erin in the jeep's passenger seat before driving out of the Blackwater Lake High School parking lot. *Go, Wolverines*, he thought as they passed the mascot displayed on the marquee.

"What makes you jump to that conclusion?" she asked.

"Because we're going to the thrift store where Brewster told you to look for a costume. That implies you're planning to go to the party."

"I am," she confirmed. "It's like Brewster said—being neighborly is a way of life. So, I want to be a good neighbor. At least while I'm here."

He kept forgetting that she was leaving. So much for watching his six. He'd better be more vigilant about protecting his perimeter or there would be hell to pay. He'd managed not to kiss her again, which wasn't easy. But necessary. Kissing would lead to sex and he had no doubt that would be as excellent as last time, but no way was it the smart move.

"So why am I shopping with you?" he asked.

"Because we're already here in town. But if you have things to do, we can go back and get my car." She looked over. "Why? What did you think? That I was going to try and convince you to go to the party?"

That's exactly what he'd thought. "Not if you're smart."

"Oh, I'm smart." Her tone was full of brash confidence. "And I'm still going to make a case for why you should go."

Jack couldn't wait to see what her strategic approach would be. "This is going to be good."

"I don't know about that, but I agree with Brewster. It's important to support the community where you live. To give back and be a part of it."

"You don't live here," he reminded her. And himself.

"For a little while longer, I do." She was quiet for a moment, probably bringing in reinforcements. "I've always lived in a good-sized city and Blackwater Lake is different. Special. It's actually possible to know everyone in town and they're people worth knowing. Your friend Danny Potter was right. This is the best place in the world. And Brewster is right, too. The magic doesn't work if you don't get involved."

Damn. That was some serious ammunition she'd hit him with. "Roger that."

"So, you're going to the party?"

"I'll take it under advisement."

"You won't regret it, Jack.

Although she was right that he didn't regret talking to the high school class, he wasn't so sure about this.

A few minutes later he pulled into the thrift-store parking lot, a stand-alone building on the outskirts of Blackwater Lake. It looked like a barn and probably had been once, but not now. The outside was painted red with white trim. There was a sign visible from the main road that said all donations welcome. All proceeds went to the Blackwater Lake Sunshine Fund.

That was right up Erin's alley. He didn't know for sure, but wouldn't be surprised if Sunshine was her middle name.

He parked the jeep, noting that there were quite a few cars in the lot. That meant a lot of people inside. Super. They exited the car and approached the wide open door.

"Isn't this place cute?" she said.

"Not the word I would use."

By the spacious entrance Erin pointed out half barrels overflowing with flowers. An old wood-and-tin washboard propped up against the outside wall. A piece of wooden ladder because everyone knew you couldn't have too many half ladders that were completely useless.

"Looks like junk to me."

"One man's trash is another man's treasure."

He looked down at the high color on her cheeks, the excitement in her eyes that made her beautiful. The feeling was like a sucker punch. "Don't you ever get tired of being an optimist?"

She shook her head. "Did you know that it takes more muscles to frown than to smile? You should try it sometime."

He'd done more of that since she showed up than he could ever remember doing in his whole life. But that information was best kept to himself.

They walked inside and let their eyes adjust to the dimness before glancing around. In his opinion it looked like a hoarder's garage exploded in here. There were mismatched dishes, suitcases, wall hangings, old bottles, a trunk, furniture. And dust. A whole lot of it.

"This is going to be so much fun."

Jack studied the bright smile of anticipation on her face and decided they should make her president in charge of the Sunshine Fund. He wanted to put on the shades he'd just slid to the top of his head. "Does your cell phone have a GPS tracker?"

"I don't know. Probably. Why?"

"If we get separated, I'll send in search-and-rescue."

"Very funny." She tsked. "Come on."

After moving down a center aisle, where they passed lamps, old toys and more ancient furniture, they found an older woman, somewhere in her late fifties or early sixties, he figured. She was still attractive and had short blond hair and brown eyes. In jeans and a thrift-store T-shirt, she was trim and friendly-looking.

"Erin." The woman's smile was warm. "Nice to see you."

"Hi, Aggie." She looked up at him. "Jack, this is Brewster's wife, Aggie."

"Ma'am." He shook the hand she held out and wondered how Erin knew her when he didn't.

As if she could read his mind, Erin said, "Aggie stops by the marina to drop off Brew's lunch when he forgets it."

"Which is pretty often," the other woman added.

"When she's there, Jack, you're mostly in hunker-down mode. Or being a hermit. Or both," Erin commented.

That sounded an awful lot like a challenge. She'd told him talking to people was fun and he should try it sometime. Now was his chance. He could be friendly and charming. It had happened once or twice before.

"It's nice to meet Brewster's better half. And it has to be said…he's a very lucky man."

"Why, thank you, Mr. Garner."

"Call me Jack." He smiled, just to show Erin he knew how.

"All right. Jack." She looked from Erin to him. "So, what brings you out of your cave today?"

The downside of a charm offensive was you had to be sociable and that meant chatting. He caught the expression in Erin's green eyes that dared him to keep this up. So, he would show her.

"As my assistant would tell you, I should be working, but I took time off to talk to Mrs. Miller's honors English class today about writing."

"Good for you, Jack." The woman nodded her approval. "Did they give you a hard time? I bet a big, strong guy like you didn't have any problem keeping them in line."

"Didn't have to. They seemed interested in what I had to say. Asked a lot of questions."

"That's wonderful."

"Speaking of questions, I have one. What is the Sunshine Fund?"

"It was Mayor Goodson-McKnight's idea." Aggie folded her arms over her chest. "It's an account funded by donations to help out a down-on-their-luck citizen or family. A kid who needs help paying for football equipment so he can participate in the sport. Someone out of work who needs groceries or money to pay utilities. The city council pays me to run the thrift store, accept and organize donations. But all proceeds above and beyond overhead go into the fund. In fact a lot of the money is raised by community events."

"Like the Halloween party?" Erin asked.

"Yes." Aggie nodded. "There's a small admittance fee and it's a potluck so there's very little operating cost. Folks have fun and money is raised for a good cause. A win-win."

"Noble undertaking," Jack agreed.

"You'll be there, won't you?"

"Affirmative." It would have been like saying no to Mrs. Santa Claus.

"Wonderful. You know it's a costume party," Aggie said.

"That's why we're here," he told her.

"Then you're going to want the clothes area," she suggested. "It's in the back right corner. And if you need any props beyond hats and jewelry, just ask."

"You can actually find stuff in here?" Jack was skeptical. "Specific items?"

"It may not look that way, but things are organized and I know where everything is."

"Understood."

"So, are you two going to do a couples costume? Romeo and Juliet? Caesar and Cleopatra? Beckett and Castle? He's that writer who solves crimes on that TV show. Since you're an author…" The older woman shrugged.

"I love that show," Erin said.

Jack was glad she fielded that because he was still trying to wrap his mind around the couples-costume remark. Why would she think that?

"We're just going to look around." Erin grinned, obviously enjoying his version of being a fish out of water.

"Have fun, you two."

In the back corner they found stands of old clothes, hats and coats. Erin started rummaging through the racks along with several other women. Since no one said hello, he was pretty sure she was not acquainted with them.

She pulled out a dress, then walked over to the headgear section. In front of a full-length mirror she put on a 1930s-era hat. Turning, she said, "I could be Bonnie Parker."

A young brunette looked up and checked her out. "That would work. And on the men's rack there's a pin-striped suit. You guys could go as Bonnie and Clyde."

Erin nodded and smiled at the other woman. "Thanks. I'll keep that in mind."

Over Jack's dead body. No pun intended.

The brunette drifted away but Little Miss Perky kept looking. She pulled a pink satin jacket out and said, "Sandy from the movie *Grease*."

A familiar redhead moved in from behind him and walked over to check it out. He didn't think Delanie Carlson ever left Bar None. "Hi, Jack."

"Who let you out?"

"As it happens, I'm the boss. And people who live in glass houses shouldn't throw stones. How did you give your computer the slip?" She smiled at Erin. "He hasn't scared you off yet?"

"I'm made of sterner stuff."

"Sassy." Delanie nodded at the pink jacket. "Then Sandy is perfect for you. All Jack needs is a black leather jacket, white T-shirt and a bucket of hair gel to be your Danny Zuko."

"What makes everyone think we're coordinating costumes?" His charm had one nerve left and this woman had picked a bad time to get on it.

"You're here together, aren't you?" Delanie asked. "That shouts couple to me. Just saying…"

Erin laughed but it sounded strained. "It's not like that. We work together. You could say we're friends. But nothing more."

"Whatever. None of my business." Delanie lifted a shoulder in a shrug.

"Seriously," Erin continued. "I won't be here that much longer."

Couples costumes did not a couple make. They worked together and it was a temporary situation. Yet another reminder was like a bucket of ice water and got his attention. It was easy to slip into complacency but also dangerous. To be a couple you had to live in the same town and they didn't. Geographic distance wasn't an insurmountable problem, but not the only one. It was impossible to be a couple by yourself. He wouldn't participate because he wasn't good at being anyone's significant other. Not even Erin's.

The Blackwater Lake community costume party was on the Saturday before Halloween. Erin dressed up as Sandy from *Grease* with the pink jacket, crisp white blouse and the tightest pair of black pants she owned since the thrift store was fresh out of leather ones. Go figure. Her hair was pulled up into a sassy ponytail and blond enough with the highlights.

Jack had pulled out his inner juvenile delinquent and put it on display. The leather jacket was battered. His white T-shirt stretched across his broad chest tight enough to make the Pink Ladies swoon. And he hadn't shaved, adding an element of danger to his Danny Zuko, a bad boy in a very good way.

He parked the jeep in the lot behind the community center, next door to city hall, where the mayor's office was located. Looking at Erin he said, "So, our deal is that when I'm bored to tears we can leave, right?"

"You won't be bored." Please, God, don't let him be bored. This was supposed to be good for him and if he ended up a wallflower it wouldn't be pretty.

"But if I am we can split." He waited for confirmation.

"There's going to be food, music, dancing. People. Remember them? You're going to have a great time."

"As you're so good at reminding me, I'm a hermit. Hermits know no one."

"*Hermit* might be an exaggeration." But not by a lot.

"No, it's on the mark." He was staring at the big building with light pouring out of the windows and people moving around inside. "A hermit, by definition, avoids large gatherings. We haven't been spotted. It would be easy to turn around and leave. No one would even notice—"

"Bite your tongue, Jack Garner. That's crazy talk. And, dare I say it? Cowardly."

"I can live with that."

Probably he could. He was a hero in the noblest sense and had served his country with distinction. There was nothing to prove. But she wanted this for him. "I already paid for our admittance."

"What if I pay you back?"

"Here's an idea. Take a risk. And look at it this way— when tonight is over you'll realize that no harm was done in this socialization experiment."

"What about my ego?"

"It's so big you won't even miss a little bit if you're dinged."

"Ouch." He opened the driver's side door. "This is a tough crowd. I think I'll take my chances with the hostiles."

"That's the spirit." She slid out, then opened the rear passenger door to retrieve the batch of four-cheese macaroni she'd made. "Love the optimism, by the way."

"Thanks." He was waiting at the front of the jeep for her. "Good talk."

"See? I proved you wrong. I am good for something. There was a time when you didn't want me here."

Spotlights on the outside of the building shone in his eyes, illuminating a sudden intensity. But it disappeared when he said in a teasing tone, "Now it's hard to picture Blackwater Lake without you in it."

Erin stumbled in her black heels but it wasn't about the uneven surface of the parking lot as much as his words.

Did he mean that or was it more to mess with her? Between that and the feel of his hand on her arm to steady her she was in a state that could best be described as flummoxed. When the buzzing in her head stopped she was going to ask whether or not he was serious, but by that time they were approaching the door. Putting the discussion on hold seemed prudent.

A woman Erin had never met was sitting at a table just inside the door. Face paint made it hard to tell her age and the black hair looked sprayed on. She was wearing an orange T-shirt with a spider and web on it and a headband with pumpkins sticking up.

She grinned at them. "Sandy and Danny. You guys look great. Name, please. I'll check my list."

"Erin Riley and Jack Garner."

"The writer." Her eyes grew as big as saucers and no reply from him was necessary since she babbled on. "I'm a big fan. Dory Carter." A little flustered, she glanced down and scanned the sheet of paper in front of her. "Here you are. I'll stamp you."

They held out their hands and came away with an inked pumpkin on the back.

"The table against the wall over there is for food," Dory said. "Just drop off your dish and have a great time. Happy Halloween."

"Thanks, Dory," she said.

The oblong-shaped room was big with long tables and folding chairs set up at one end. The walls had pictures of witches, ghosts and vampires. White cottony web with spiders caught in it was liberally spread over everything. Orange and black balloons decorated the tables. It was cheerful and festive. They took the casserole dish containing a double batch of four-cheese macaroni to the food table and Jack set it down. "Mission accomplished."

"Come on, Captain America, let's mingle." She snapped her fingers. "Now that would have been a fitting costume."

"I don't do tights."

"I'm not sure he does them, either." She pointed. "There's the sheriff. That's a good place to start being sociable. He's already your friend."

"April Kennedy is with him."

"Look at this as an opportunity to show her you're not a temperamental writer."

"I'm not."

"If you say so."

Side by side they threaded their way through the crowd to where the couple was standing. Will Fletcher was in his sheriff's uniform and his fiancée had on an orange jumpsuit.

"Hi," Erin greeted them. She looked at the man's khaki shirt and pants. "I thought costumes were mandatory. You're cheating."

"I'm on duty. Crowd control." He grinned down at the woman beside him. "And this is Shady Sadie, my prisoner."

"Prisoner of love," she said, grinning at him before looking them over. "And you guys look great."

"It's all her." Jack nodded in Erin's direction.

"Thanks goes to the thrift store. The Sunshine Fund is a little sunnier now."

Jack looked around the room that was getting more crowded all the time. "Is it always like this?"

"Yes," April said. "People in this town do holidays right and Halloween is neck and neck with Christmas as the favorite. Who doesn't love to get dressed up and be someone they're not?"

Erin gave Jack a look that warned him not to say that under protest *he* was dressed up and pretending to be someone he wasn't. His small smile said that's exactly what he'd planned to say but he got the message.

"There are some very creative costumes," April said, letting her gaze wander over the people closest to them. "And some…not so much. Seriously? A shirt that says *This is my costume*?"

"Nobody cares." Will was constantly looking, checking things out. "Mostly we just love a good excuse for a party."

Jack was watching the other man, alpha male to alpha male. "Must be hard on you having to work."

"Not so bad. I'm a trained observer and do it all the time whether I'm on the clock or not. This way my staff gets to relax and let their hair down. And tonight I get paid."

"And I get paid to take pictures." April removed a small camera from the pocket of her jumpsuit. "Let's get one of our local celebrity. Say cheese, you two."

Without warning, Jack pulled her into his arms and bent her back, as if getting ready to kiss her. There was a flash and Erin wasn't sure if it was the camera or his grin. Before she could decide, he stood up straight and brought her with him, keeping his arm around her waist. It was very coupley and nice. But she was pretty sure he was messing with her.

April was checking out the shot. "Good move, Jack. Great picture of you both."

"Happy to oblige."

"This one is going to make it into the newspaper," the photographer proclaimed.

"What?" Jack tensed a little.

April looked up. "Like I said, I get paid to take pictures. I do freelance work along with having my shop. The *Blackwater Lake Review Journal* pays me for any pictures they print. I hope it's okay to submit this one for consideration."

"Absolutely." The smile Jack aimed at the other woman oozed charm.

"Good." She snapped her fingers. "Speaking of that... There's someone you need to meet."

Erin watched her disappear into the crowd. "Where is she going?"

"No idea," Will answered. "It's always an adventure when you hang out with a creative personality. But you should be used to that."

Maybe. But she was resisting that feeling because hanging out with Jack was going to end sooner rather than later.

April reappeared with a nice-looking man in his thirties who was wearing a black Stetson, worn jeans, a long-sleeved snap-front shirt and boots. Best guess? This was a cowboy costume, although there were enough people who made their living on ranches around here that it was hard to tell.

"Jack, I want you to meet Logan Turner, owner, publisher and editor of our local paper. Logan, this is Jack Garner and his research assistant, Erin Riley."

"I'm a big fan of your work." Logan held out his hand. "It's a pleasure to meet you."

"Same here."

"Look, Jack..." He hesitated, then barreled on. "I'm just going to put this out there and feel free to tell me to go to hell. I know you don't do interviews. Although lack of promotion didn't seem to hurt the sales of your book any. But I was wondering if you'd make an exception and talk to me for an article. Now that you've put down roots here in Blackwater Lake."

"How do you know I have?"

Logan shrugged. "Heard about the talk you did for the high school kids."

Erin felt a knot in her stomach the size of Montana.

Chapter Twelve

The party broke up just after midnight and Jack drove the jeep out of the community center parking lot. If this was a fairy tale he would be in a pumpkin right now. Kind of appropriate for Halloween. And it was conspicuously quiet on the passenger side of this pumpkin so he waited for incoming. Some form of I-told-you-so. It didn't take long and he grinned when she cleared her throat.

"So, let's debrief," she began.

"Like a military operation?"

"Yes. Were you bored tonight?"

He knew one-word answers made her crazy and making this easy on her wasn't his plan. "No."

"At any point during the evening did you feel the urge to bail because you were not being intellectually challenged?"

"Does now count?"

"No. This is not bailing," she informed him. "It's called closing the place down."

"Then no." There was silence from the other seat. "What's wrong?"

"I forgot the question." She sounded a little tipsy.

"Then I'll remind you. You asked whether I felt the need to bail because I was bored."

"Right. Did you?"

"No."

"Isn't there something you want to tell me?" she asked.

"Many things." He knew what she wanted to hear and wasn't going to play.

"Don't make me hurt you, Jack."

He laughed. "Bring it."

"Okay. Watching you tonight was like seeing a butterfly escape the cocoon."

"Dramatic much?"

"It's not drama if you're dead serious. And I am. You opened up. Like peeling away another layer of an onion."

"Metaphors must be on sale tonight," he said wryly.

She ignored the jab and went on. "You were downright friendly in there. Could have knocked me over with a feather when you agreed to an interview for the paper."

"I'm always friendly."

There was a moment of stunned silence before she started to laugh. "Oh my God. That's too funny. The first time we met I thought you were going to pick me up bodily and throw me off the porch."

"I thought about it."

"Seriously?"

"Of course not," he said.

"Oh. I get it. That was to distract me, make me lose my train of thought before making my point. But I'm on to you." She scoffed. "You were charming and funny tonight. People like you and you made friends. It's a victory."

"One skirmish. That's all."

"It was more than that. I saw the way women were looking at you."

"Not interested." Because none of them was her. The thought popped into his mind and blew up like an improvised explosive device.

"Okay. Maybe that's pushing the socialization experiment too far." There was a *but* in the air. *Wait for it...* "But you seemed to get along really well with the guys."

"Seriously?"

"I'm always serious." She was thinking. He could feel it.

"Let me list those guys for you," she said. "There was the sheriff. Sloan Holden and his cousin, Burke. Maggie's brother Brady. And don't tell me you were putting up a front because this is me. I know you're not that good an actor."

"They seem like stand-up guys," he admitted.

"And?"

"What?" He wished she would just drop it.

"Just tell me I was right and you had fun." There was frustration in her tone.

"Now whose ego needs a jump start?"

"Jack—"

He laughed. "Okay."

"So you're glad you went," she prompted.

"Don't push it—"

There was a big sigh from her side of the car. "Why do you make it so hard? Why can't you just give it up and admit that I was right? Would it be so bad to open up a little?"

"Because I'm a warrior, trained to resist."

He was teasing, but the words stuck in his head and wouldn't let go. Once burned, you pushed back and established a safe zone to keep from being hurt again.

Outside the Blackwater Lake city limit it was pitch-black without the commercial lights of town. There was nothing but darkness beyond the range of the jeep's headlights. They were alone. She couldn't see his face; he couldn't see hers. And suddenly he wanted to tell her why he'd closed himself off.

"Do you remember when you asked me if I had a girlfriend or was married?"

"Yes. You said there wasn't anyone."

"Not now." Except for the feelings rattling around inside of him for Erin and she didn't fit into either of those categories. It felt like a lie to leave them unsaid, but that's the only way he knew to protect her. "I was married once."

"So, you're divorced." She wasn't asking.

"I think that's what 'married once but not now' means."

He gave her a wry look and didn't know whether or not she could see it in the dim interior.

"Right. Of course." She blew out a long breath. "It's just that was unexpected. More peeling of the onion. My comment was meant to encourage an exchange of information. And I'm officially babbling. Please feel free to interrupt me at any time and continue peeling the onion, so to speak."

She made him smile, which was a minor miracle, what with the dark memories he'd voluntarily given up. "I met a woman in a bar."

"Not a surprise. Apparently that's where you meet all your friends," she said dryly.

"She wasn't a friend. Do you want to hear this or not?"

"Sorry. I'm listening. Please continue."

Jack gripped the steering wheel a little tighter. "It turned into a thing pretty fast. We got married before my first deployment. There's something about facing danger that makes you want to have someone waiting for you when you get back."

"How long were you married?"

"Ten years. But only because I was deployed a lot. When I left the army she left me."

"I'm sorry, Jack. That must have hurt you a lot."

The genuine sympathy in her voice touched him almost as if she'd put her hand on his arm. It was like healing salve to an open wound. "I'm over it."

"Are you?"

"What does that mean?" Stupid question. He knew what she was getting at and was sorry he'd started this in the first place. "Never mind. My question was rhetorical."

"Mine wasn't. You have a point and I'd like to hear what it is."

Jack slowed the jeep for a left-hand turn onto Lakeshore Drive. They were almost home. His home, not hers. She was temporary.

In a few moments the lights from the porch and the marina beyond came into view. He pulled up beside Erin's rental car and parked. When he switched off the ignition there was an eerie silence.

Erin undid her seat belt and angled her knees toward him. "Jack? What is it you wanted to say?"

Without answering he released his own seat belt and got out of the car, then headed for the porch. Sounds behind him indicated she was hot on his heels. She caught up to him just as he unlocked the front door and opened it. Harley barked and bounded outside. He circled them, completely joyful that his humans had returned.

This human wanted to exfiltrate the situation ASAP. He pushed the door wider and started to walk into the house.

"Wait, Jack." This time she did put her hand on his arm.

He wanted to strip off the leather jacket and feel the gentle touch on his bare skin. "Let it go. Trust me, I'm no hero."

"Isn't that for me to decide?"

Who was he kidding? From the moment she first showed up on this very porch she'd proven she wasn't a quitter. There was no reason to believe that had changed. "You're not going to let this slide, are you?"

"Not until you get to the point."

"Okay. Don't forget you asked for it." He saw the concern on her face and it was too damn close to pity for his liking. *Get this over with.* "I was a teenage delinquent. Big disappointment to my mother. I was a crappy husband and my marriage was a bust. So I was two for two. And failure doesn't sit well with me. My point is that I'm no good at relationships, so avoiding them is a win."

"You only fail when you fail to try," she said so softly he almost didn't hear.

"Did you get that from a motivational seminar?"

"From my weight-loss support group, actually. But you were saying…"

"I'm only good at being a soldier. I don't want to let anyone else down. The best way to achieve that goal is keeping to myself."

"Cut yourself a break, Jack. Exercise those friendship muscles. Just do it. You might surprise yourself."

He didn't get her. He just didn't. Anyone else would have given up on him by now. Thrown in the towel and said good riddance. But she was hanging in there and it was both annoying and astonishing. "Why is it so important to you that I insert myself into this town?"

"Because I don't want you to be all alone when I'm gone." Her gaze searched his face as she caught her top lip between her teeth.

The words were like an explosion in his heart and looking at her mouth tore his willpower to shreds. He wanted her more than his next breath and talking was optional. After pulling her inside and shutting the door, Jack took her in his arms and kissed her. He poured all the feelings there were no words for into the kiss…making it one eloquent kiss. Show, don't tell.

Erin melted against him like chocolate left out in the sun. Or ice cream in the oven. He was right. A sale on metaphors tonight. A *fire* sale. This was a bad idea, but when it felt so good how was that wrong?

Jack tasted like pumpkin cinnamon spice—the cake he'd eaten at the potluck. His lips were soft, warm and full of temptation, but part of her was still resisting, right up until he tenderly freed her hair from the ponytail and let it fall over her shoulders. He wasn't fooling around. Well, he was, in the best possible way.

When she stood on tiptoe and settled her arms around his neck, he put his hands under her butt and easily lifted her. She wrapped her legs around his waist and he headed for the hallway where the bedrooms were located. His? Hers? Erin didn't care just as long as it had a bed. She kissed his lips, cheek, neck and earlobe.

The last kiss touched a nerve and he groaned, tightening his arms around her. "You're playing with fire."

"Do I have your attention?"

"Oh, yeah."

He was breathing hard and she hoped it wasn't the extra pounds that refused to budge from her thighs. "I'm too heavy, Jack."

He stopped underneath the hall light and his eyes glittered with intensity. "Let's get one thing straight."

"If this is going to be a long discussion, you might want to put me down first. Your back will thank you."

Very slowly he shook his head. "About that weight-loss support group you mentioned? Waste of time. You don't need it."

"Really?"

"Affirmative." A slow, sexy smile curved up the corners of his mouth. "Your body is perfect."

"Then you have pretty low standards. My legs are too short and—"

His mouth quickly and efficiently stopped the flow of her words and had warmth pooling in her belly. And then he was on the move again, turning right into his bedroom. He stopped beside the king-size bed and set her on her feet before sliding his hands to her waist. He pulled the white blouse from the waistband of her black pants. His fingers brushed the bare, sensitive skin beneath and a moan escaped.

It was like throwing kerosene on a campfire. She pushed at his shirt and her pink jacket ended up on the floor beside his black leather one. In ten seconds flat they were naked and he tugged her to him, settling his big palms on her rear end again. He lifted, letting her wrap her legs around him before bracing a knee on the mattress and gently setting her in the center.

The muscles in his arms and chest flexed, making her want to swoon, so it was a good thing she was already down. He reached into the nightstand drawer and felt around before finally pulling out a condom.

He frowned at her laugh. "Something funny?"

"Who knew condoms are like smoke detectors. You have one in every room." She smiled up at him. "Not complaining, just saying…"

"You talk too much."

"It's a flaw. I'm working on it—"

His mouth silenced her for the second time as he kissed her thoroughly. By the time he moved his attention to her neck, then lower to her breast, she was too caught up in the delicious sensations to say a word.

Jack nibbled his way over her abdomen, hip and thigh until she was writhing with need, her body begging for release. He moved his body over hers, then thrust gently inside and she arched her hips to meet him. Her breathing grew more labored as he slowly moved in and out, taking her higher.

Without warning the tension inside her stretched and snapped, sending shock waves of exquisite pleasure thorough every part of her. She splintered into a thousand points of light and he held her until she came back together.

He rolled to his back, taking her with him so that she was on top. She rested her cheek on his chest, delighting in the way his heart thundered beneath her ear. When she shifted her hips against him, once then twice, he groaned and went still, wrapping her tightly against him while he found his own release. They stayed locked together for a very long time.

The last thing Erin wanted to do was move. She'd never felt this safe with a man, not even with her fiancé before he got sick. That thought opened the flood gates and let the guilt flow unchecked. It also opened the door to all the things she didn't want to face.

"I have to go—"

Jack didn't loosen his hold. "Don't leave on my account."

The warmth of his skin and the security of his arms were intoxicating, like a drug she craved. All the more reason she needed to break the contact.

"Let me go, Jack."

He brushed a big hand down her back before rolling over with her beneath him. Gently he touched his mouth to hers. "I'm going to get up—"

"Okay, then I can—"

He touched a finger to her lips. "I'll be right back. I don't want you to move."

"Okay." But she couldn't look at him.

"Promise, Erin." He nudged her chin up, just enough so that their gazes locked and he could see into hers. "Give me your word."

Good grief he was stubborn. It was a strength and a flaw. Right up there with being too perceptive because she'd planned to make her escape. But clearly it was important to him that she didn't.

She nodded. "I'll stay. Promise."

When he left her and went into the bathroom she felt exposed in so many ways. Pulling the sheet up over her nakedness only helped a little. Before she had time to blow everything out of proportion he was back and lifting that sheet to slide into bed beside her. Then he put an arm under her and folded her next to his warm body. It was a wonderful place to be.

"So, I was thinking—"

"Uh-oh. That can't be good. You might want to shut that down ASAP." She was joking. Mostly.

"Just hear me out."

"Oddly enough, those words aren't making me feel any better."

"Keep an open mind."

"Still not making me feel better," she said, hoping he wouldn't say whatever was on his mind. Somehow she knew it was going to complicate things even more than they already were.

"Sometimes I wish you weren't quite so verbal." The beginnings of frustration tinged his words.

"It's a gift."

"And a curse." But he settled his chin on the top of her

hair. "The thing is, I don't see any reason you can't move into my bed."

Erin's heart skipped a beat, then started up again, pounding very hard. She didn't know how to respond to that. Saying nothing seemed the best way to keep from saying something wrong.

"Or I'll move into your bed," he offered.

That's how he'd interpreted her silence?

"For the duration of our collaboration." He waited for an answer that didn't come. Obviously he noted her less-than-enthusiastic reaction to his suggestion. "Erin?"

"I heard you."

"It makes sense if you think about it." He was going into close-the-deal mode. "We like each other. We're friends."

With benefits. But she kept that thought to herself.

"There's no reason we shouldn't enjoy each other for the next couple of weeks. Until this joint venture is over. What do you say?"

"No."

"Good, I—" The single word seemed to penetrate and he said, "What?"

"Negative on moving into your bed or mine."

She should slip out of his arms now and try to pull her dignity together to make a graceful exit. Or escape. The second option would be more accurate. But she wanted to hang on to this intimacy just a little longer.

"Is it necessary for me to point out that this is the second time we've had sex?"

"I'm well aware of that," she said.

"Okay." Absently he rubbed a strand of her hair between his fingers. "The first time you could chalk it up to…impulsiveness."

"Now who's being verbal. This is very uncharacteristic of you, Jack." The rumble of his laugh vibrated in his chest, tickling her cheek.

"But the second time it's more difficult to make a case for spontaneity. It's leaning toward a pattern," he pointed out.

"I reject the word *pattern*. It comes under the heading of 'moment of weakness.'"

"Twice," he reminded her. "And that tips into pattern territory if you ask me."

"No one asked."

"Erin—"

She sat up and slid away from him. "Look, Jack, we know what this is and isn't. In the long run it's better not to take that step. I've learned not to make decisions in haste."

Before he could say anything else that might weaken her resolve, she got out of bed, gathered up her clothes and left his room. She scurried across the hall into her own and shut the door firmly behind her.

Holding her breath, she waited for him to knock. To follow her and try to change her mind, part of her hoping he wouldn't let her go that easily.

But there was nothing. Only silence.

And when there was silence her mind had the freedom to work overtime. She wasn't ashamed of sleeping with him. But how was she ever going to face him in the morning?

Chapter Thirteen

The next morning when Erin didn't show up for their status meeting by five minutes after nine Jack was officially concerned. Last night he'd had probably the best sex of his life. He would freely admit that blood flow to his brain hadn't yet returned to normal when he suggested changing their sleeping arrangements. It was quite possible he hadn't made it clear that sex wasn't the reason. Not the only one, anyway. He was a guy after all.

But he wanted her close. The smell of her skin, the warmth of her body. Something about her made everything brighter, more peaceful, and God knew there hadn't been enough peace in his life.

If he'd said any of that she would have thought he was crazy. Or laughed at him waxing poetic, which might just have been worse. Instead, she gave him a negative and told him she'd learned not to make hasty decisions. He wasn't used to hearing no, but ego had nothing to do with anything. At least not much.

What made him uneasy was that Erin was nothing if not prompt. And stubborn. She'd gone to the mat for her stupid morning meeting. Until she hadn't shown up, he didn't realize how much he'd started looking forward to seeing her for those few minutes after breakfast, before he started working on the book. The one he wrote during the day.

Breakfast had been simple this morning. Eggs, potatoes, toast, fruit, coffee. But the woman who'd cooked it was stewing about something and no work was getting done until he made sure she was okay.

"Harley, walk."

The dog yipped out a bark and scurried over to the office door, waiting expectantly, giving no indication that he'd noticed their walk usually happened a lot later in the day.

Jack picked up his pet and scratched beneath the furry chin. "I don't think I've ever told you how much I appreciate the fact that you aren't complicated."

The dog licked his face.

"You're welcome. Let's go find Erin." One bark signaled the animal's solidarity with that plan.

He carried Harley down the stairs and set him on the porch, knowing he would take off running. Before following, Jack took a quick look in the house, then made sure her rental car was still parked beside the jeep. It wasn't gone, which meant she was on foot as he'd suspected. Private eye Mac Daniels had nothing on him.

Jack started jogging down the path beside the lake to catch up to his dog. About half a mile past the marina he saw Erin, down on one knee scratching and rubbing Harley, who was in doggy heaven. Not a surprise. What was not to like? There was no telling whether or not they'd caught her returning.

Jack slowed to a walk, then stopped beside them. "Hi."

She didn't look up but kept lavishing attention on the little beast she clearly had changed her mind about. "Who's a good dog?"

"You didn't used to think so."

"That was before I got to know him."

Jack waited for more. With Erin there always was, but not this time. Her silence was like the quiet in a war zone before the world exploded all to hell. Waiting was the worst part. This time he could call the shots.

"Now that you know him, what makes you like him?"

"He's loyal, obedient, understanding and loves unconditionally. He doesn't expect anything in return."

"So looks has nothing to do with it."

"It's all about character," she agreed.

Jack had the feeling she wasn't talking about the dog anymore. "They say dogs are a reflection of their owners."

"Seems like I've heard that." She looked up then. "I'm not so sure about that in his case. He's not especially abrasive or short—" She laughed when the *he* in question batted her with a paw to let her know he wanted more attention. "That is, he's short but in a noble way."

"He lets you know what he needs. Never have to guess." Last night for instance. She'd implied what they'd done was a moment of weakness. A mistake. He couldn't disagree more and it bugged him that she thought so.

"It's a good quality," she said. "Along with honesty—"

Jack heard the catch in her voice and felt the emotion of it without a clue what was going on. There was a time when her perkiness annoyed him, but not now. He'd give anything for her to challenge him with words and the fire in her green eyes that he'd come to expect when she was making a point.

"What's wrong, Erin?"

"Just tired, I guess."

Frustration tightened in his gut. He was no expert on women, but was pretty sure *tired* was the same as saying nothing was bothering her. "I've seen you tired and this isn't it."

"Really, I'm fine."

He hated that word. Every man on the planet hated that word when a woman looked the way she did and said it in the tone she'd used. Both were clues that she was the exact opposite of fine.

Jack picked up a stick and got the dog's attention. He threw it and the animal tensed, waiting for permission. "Harley, fetch."

The dog took off like a shot, eager to obey the order. If only it was that easy to understand this woman. "You're not okay. Or you wouldn't have missed the nine-o'clock status meeting. The one you insisted on, in case you forgot."

"I didn't." She stood up and met his gaze. "It doesn't seem all that important anymore."

Negative, he thought. Maybe she didn't realize, but that was when he fleshed out and fine-tuned the scene he was working on. He'd taken her suggestion to write about Harley and it had gone in a different direction, one that would never see the light of day. That writing happened at night and was personal in a way Mac Daniels would never be.

Bottom line: their status-meeting chats were responsible for moving the book forward and it was almost finished.

"You're wrong," he said. "They are important."

"I stand corrected. My bad." She looked down for a moment. "Let's go back and we can talk about the book on the way."

"Forget the book."

"I can't. It's my job," she reminded him.

"And it's my career. But I didn't follow you because of some damn arbitrary schedule."

"Then why did you follow me?"

"Because—" He blew out a breath. "I made a suggestion last night after we—"

"Slept together." She met his gaze directly.

He remembered the first day she'd walked with him and the look on her face when he'd challenged whether or not she could do the job without looking at him as if she wanted him to take her to bed. She sure wasn't looking at him that way right now because of what happened last night. And if he had to guess, he would say she looked ashamed. He had to fix that.

"We slept together," he said. "You need to know that meant a lot to me."

"I appreciate you saying that, Jack." The corners of her mouth curved up but it was a sad smile.

Where was the GPS when you really needed it? He was in uncharted territory and could use some coordinates to head him in the right direction. "Do I need to apologize? If I was out of line—"

"Stop. This isn't about you, Jack."

"Well, it can't be about you. You're practically perfect. Never abrasive. A little short maybe, but no one can hold your DNA against you." He was trying to get a smile out of her but with zero results so far. "Look, you're the one who stuck it out with your fiancé after a cancer diagnosis. I don't know any woman who, under those circumstances, would keep the ring. But you did. Until the end."

"Stop," she said again. "I'm not that nice for staying when he got sick. I'm an impostor."

He must be missing a piece of this puzzle. "Let me get

this straight. He was dying and you didn't leave. You loved him until the end. How is that a bad thing?"

She looked more guilt-ridden with every word and winced at the word *love*. "The truth is I wasn't in love with him. I realized it and was trying to figure out how to break the news that my feelings had changed when he got even worse news. I loved him as a friend and couldn't walk out when he needed me."

"Okay. Still not seeing the bad."

"More than once he brought up the subject of a small wedding, but I always came up with some lame excuse. Wait until chemo was over and he would be in remission. Then he was too weak and didn't bring it up anymore." She shrugged. "On paper we were a perfect match. Both teachers who wanted to see the world. That was about having something in common, not love. I jumped in too soon when I accepted his proposal. If he hadn't gotten sick I would have broken it off."

The bleak look in her eyes made Jack want to pull her into his arms, but he was afraid if he touched her she would shatter. "First, you're being too hard on yourself."

"You're wrong, I—"

He held up a hand to stop her. "You said what you had to and now it's my turn."

"Okay."

"Second, let me give you a guy's perspective. It would have been more dishonest to take vows. He probably knew the truth and was pretending, too, because it would have been harder being alone. You call it dishonest, I call it courageous."

There was moisture in her eyes but she blinked it away. "Maybe someday I'll share your opinion."

"Believe it. I do."

"About last night—" She caught the corner of her lip between her teeth then met his gaze. "I like you, Jack."

"So you said last night."

"That was completely honest. With my fiancé I jumped in too fast and stayed for the wrong reason. If I moved into your bed, that would be jumping in too fast when we both know I'm not staying. As mistakes go, that would be the bigger one."

As opposed to the mistake of having sex.

Jack had to admit she had him there. He didn't like it but she had him. Before he could think of a comeback, she nodded and walked past him, heading back to the house. Harley followed her and Jack couldn't blame him.

This was a sneak preview of what he would get on her last day with him. Watching her leave. He didn't much like the view. And now there was the devil to pay. He found out what was eating her, that she felt dishonest for not telling a dying man she wasn't in love with him.

Oddly enough that made Jack trust her more. And want her in his bed even more than that. The problem with what she'd confessed was that it took the wanting to a level he'd never experienced before. A place it wasn't safe to be.

It was entirely possible that he wouldn't survive Erin Riley after all.

Erin put the finishing touches on breakfast and thought about Jack calling her out on missing their meeting yesterday. She had to own taking the coward's way out. It was always the best course of action to face an issue head-on, but she'd headed in the opposite direction. Then he'd tracked her down, kept her honest. Confessing her guilt about not loving Garrett seemed to lift the burden that she'd carried since his death. Jack's words gave her absolution and she would always be grateful. She'd also told him she wouldn't share his bed because she had to leave.

He hadn't tried to change her mind.

What she felt for him was much more than just *like* and if he'd only said "don't go" it would have been enough. But he hadn't. Still, the air was cleared and things went back to normal. Whatever that was. Jack acted as if nothing happened so she would, too. She only had two weeks left so there was no point in rocking the boat.

"What's for breakfast?"

Speaking of the devil, there he was in the doorway. Because winter was coming fast, this morning he was wearing a long-sleeved black T-shirt with his jeans. It was a good look, but then he didn't have a bad one. When he was near, her heart pounded erratically no matter what he was wearing. Or not wearing. Maybe she should rethink that offer to share his bed…

"Erin?"

"Hmm?"

"Breakfast?" He moved closer and looked at what she was doing. "French toast."

"You're quite the detective."

"Not me, but I'm writing one."

"How's that going?" She dragged a slice of bread through the egg mixture and dropped it in the frying pan. The grease was a little hotter than she thought and it splattered. "Whoa—"

"Careful." He hovered, ready to intervene. "You okay?"

"Fine. Watch out or you'll get burned."

"Too late."

Instantly her gaze lifted to his, but he quickly shuttered any expression and she had no idea what he'd meant. Burned by his wife? By her? Or he'd literally felt splashes of hot oil just now. Change of subject.

She'd heard him in his office again last night. He was putting in a lot of time, a good sign about significant progress on his sequel.

She added three more slices of bread to the frying pan. "So, how's Mac Daniels these days?"

"I'll save that for the status meeting. You'll be there, right?"

"Wouldn't miss it." Not again.

She had already put the bottle of syrup on the table along with cut-up fruit. When the toast was evenly browned and crispy, she put a slice on her plate and the rest on Jack's. After handing them to him, she grabbed the platter of bacon. "Let's eat."

"I'm starved."

He always was. She was going to miss cooking for him—because he seemed to appreciate good food. Going back to meals for one was a sad, lonely and pathetic thought so she gave herself permission to run away just this once and made a conscious decision not to face it until she had to.

Erin sat down across from him and picked up her fork and knife. She cut a bite and chewed thoughtfully. "The weather is turning cold."

"You're not in Phoenix anymore."

"I noticed." She spooned some fruit on her plate. "What is it like here in the winter?"

"Cold. Snow. Tourists come for ski season." He shrugged.

"There will probably be more people now with the new hotel opening and the condos for sale near the mountain." She got all the news when shopping for groceries in town. "The newspaper is full of information about business expansion."

"That reminds me. Logan Turner called. I'm going to meet him later for the interview."

"You should let Cheryl know. That will make her happy."

Jack picked up a crispy piece of bacon and there was a twinkle in his eyes. "Maybe we should see how it goes before I tell my editor. If he critiques my characterization of women or talks about the next book it won't be pretty."

"You are many things, Jack, but dumb as dirt is not one of them. I believe you're capable of learning from your—"

"Mistakes?" One dark eyebrow lifted.

"I was going to say missteps."

"Same thing."

"But it sounds so much better. You can trust me on that," she teased.

"Yeah." The words pushed the laughter from his expression and replaced it with a smoky intensity.

"Do you want me there for the interview?"

"To keep me on the straight and narrow?"

"Moral support," she said to clarify.

"It's not technically in your job description, but…yeah, I'd appreciate it if you had my back."

"Of course I do."

While they talked he ate and finished all of his French toast. "Did I mention that this is really good?"

"No." The unexpected compliment from this particular man made her warm and gooey inside. "But thanks. I'm glad you like it."

Because there wouldn't be many more. Erin didn't say that out loud, but the thought stayed in the air between them.

They finished their coffee, but it seemed to take longer than usual. Then she glanced at the time and reluctantly stood and grabbed their plates.

"Time to get to work."

He nodded. "I'll go upstairs and get organized."

"I'll be there by nine," she said.

"Promises, promises." He grinned, then turned and left the kitchen. Moments later the front door closed.

Without moving Erin stared at the place where he'd just been standing. She felt blinded by the brightness of that smile, so different from the hard-faced man he'd been the first time they met. This man was going to leave a mark on her heart.

But there was no time to dwell on what she couldn't change. As quickly as possible she did the dishes then wiped down the kitchen table and counters. When all was as shiny and bright as Jack's smile, she went out the front door and up the stairs to his office.

After knocking once she went inside and saw him behind his desk. She saluted and said, "Reporting for duty, sir."

The corners of his mouth curved up. "The salute needs work."

"So does this room." She frowned at the stacks of paper on his desk and file folders placed haphazardly on every flat surface, including the floor. Had it been this bad yesterday when she came up here after their conversation? She wasn't sure. Apparently that talk had put her in a fog, but she'd bet that it was now officially worse than she'd ever seen. He must have been very busy last night. "You call this organized?"

Jack calmly surveyed the chaos surrounding him. "I know where everything is."

"Hmm." She settled her hands on her hips. "It doesn't strike you as the tiniest bit hypocritical that you were skeptical when Aggie said she knew where everything in the thrift store was?"

"No."

"Of course not." She sighed.

"Don't worry about it."

She moved closer. "Someone has to. How in the world do you concentrate in here?"

"One way to look at this is motivation to be in a world of my own creation."

"I hope your imaginary world is tidier than this one," she said ruefully. "Seriously, it must take you forever to find anything?"

"At this point in the book I don't need to. All the research is in the manuscript and I scroll through as necessary."

"Then why not put it away?"

"No reason. Habit. My process." He leaned his forearms on the desk. "So, are we done with this topic? Mac is in crisis."

"He's not the only one," she muttered.

"I heard that."

"Sorry." She moved a pile of folders to the floor in order to sit in her customary chair facing the desk. "Is he trying to decide whether to go after the dirty bomb or the bad guy?"

"No. He's thinking he made a mistake hiring someone to answer the phones in his new office."

"Since he just set up shop, I'm guessing it doesn't yet look like an office supply store threw up in it."

"Focus." He was enjoying this.

"Okay. What is he questioning about his hire? Is she young? Too young for him? Old? Experienced or not? Pretty? A temptation? In danger?"

"Wow. I'm almost sorry I said anything." He sat back, looking shell-shocked. "All of that off the top of your head?"

"Yeah. That's my job." She crossed one leg over the

other. "The thing is you need to make some decisions about…what's her name?"

He thought for a moment. "Let's call her Winnie."

"Short for Winifred? Seriously? Because you don't like her in particular? Or women in general. No offense to anyone with the name."

"Watch it. There's that whole characterization-of-women thing. The name is arbitrary."

"True, but what you call her can define character."

"Point taken." He rubbed his hands over his face. "So, in your opinion are there any other things I should think about for Winnie?"

"Is she going to be a recurring character? Does Mac have a history with her? Maybe she's a down-on-her-luck stranger with no skills that Mac hired out of the goodness of his heart."

"He doesn't have a heart," Jack said wryly.

She grinned. "Her life might be an open book or there could be skeletons in her closet."

"My head is spinning—"

"Maybe she's an ex-con who did time for manslaughter. Or she—"

He held up a hand to stop her. "Hold it."

"All I'm saying is she can be as simple or multilayered as you want. Just don't limit yourself with too many hard-and-fast facts if you decide that she'll be a recurring character."

He blew out a breath and stood, then started to pace. "That's a lot to think about."

"No pressure, but this is going to be a long-running series. The direction you go is important."

"Yeah. I can see that." He stopped and met her gaze. "I'm going for a run."

She stood to face him. "I didn't mean to complicate this for you."

"No. You're right. I just need to clear my head before it explodes. I won't be long."

"Is there anything you want me to research?"

"Yeah, now that you mention it. Classic literary secretaries. To avoid minefields, better known as clichés. Meet me back here in an hour."

"Roger that."

He grinned again, then went out the door with Harley hot on his heels.

Erin walked downstairs, set up her laptop on the kitchen table and pulled up what she could find on TV and movie secretaries or executive assistants. After an hour, she went back upstairs and knocked once before entering. Jack wasn't at his desk.

"Hello?"

There was no answer, which told her he hadn't returned yet. She'd printed out a lot of research pages for him and looked, without success, for an uncluttered place to put it. Temptation to tidy up his office had her fingers itching even though she remembered what he'd said that very first morning after she'd arrived. About a man's office being sacred. But an hour ago he'd said he didn't need any of this stuff so where was the harm?

She wouldn't do much. Just the little table by his desk. She took the files on top and put them neatly in the corner filing cabinet. There were loose papers underneath and she rifled through them, some of which were drawings. Of a dog that looked a lot like Harley. Jack was creative with more than just words.

Beneath the stack of drawings was another file labeled Adventures of Harley the Wonder Dog. Flipping through it she saw a compilation of charming stories that could only be targeted for children. Tales of a Chinese crested dog who compels a young boy to confront bullying. Other ones about bravery, friendship and loyalty. The writing was completely captivating. And that's the reason she never heard Jack open the office door.

"What the hell are you doing?"

Chapter Fourteen

"Jack—" Heart pounding, Erin stared at the man in the doorway. "I didn't hear you come in."

"Obviously. I repeat—what the hell are you doing with my stuff?"

She glanced at the file in her hand, the one she'd been so absorbed in that she didn't know he was there. "I did the research and printed out a bunch of information. You'd be surprised how much material there is on fictional secretaries." She was babbling. "Anyway, there was no place to put it."

"So you decided to read my private file?" His eyes narrowed and a muscle jerked in his jaw.

Some part of her mind registered that he'd taken a shower after running. His hair was damp and he'd changed into worn jeans and another long-sleeved T-shirt with ARMY in bold black letters on the front. It was as if someone had correctly dressed him for a movie scene. He was in full warrior mode and so not happy.

"You make it sound as if this was premeditated," she said. "It wasn't like that."

"I don't care how it was. The fact is you're looking at something that I didn't give you permission to read."

"The fact is," she countered, "you haven't given me permission to read very much of anything."

"So you went rogue, behind my back, to read this? That's not even part of your job description."

"Okay. Then tell me what it is."

"Nothing."

"Oh, please, Jack. You were an elite soldier trained to remain calm in combat situations when the average person would freak out and come unglued. But you're unglued now over this?" Defiantly she held up the file. "Don't insult my intelligence and tell me it's nothing."

"Don't insult mine by claiming what you're doing is cleaning up." His hands balled into fists at his sides. "You're looking through my stuff. That's called snooping."

"I was putting things in order," she said, defending herself. "Then I snooped."

She was hoping a confession laced with humor would bring his intensity down a notch, but couldn't have been more wrong. He looked angrier, if that was possible. More disturbing was how clipped his voice had been and the fact that now he wasn't saying anything at all. Since she'd first arrived he'd gone from a man of few words to downright chatty. He actually bantered with her, which was her favorite thing. But he wasn't doing it now.

"Jack, this is the truth… I was rearranging the stack of papers beside your desk and I saw this file—Adventures of Harley the Wonder Dog. How was I supposed to resist that? I was curious. So sue me. I read them and the stories are wonderful."

He simply stared at her.

"Every one has a message, a lesson, a take-away. For instance, the little boy with no friends that Harley latches on to, paving the way with other kids. Or the child who's being bullied, then rescued by a small, funny-looking dog." His expression didn't soften. If anything it got darker. "The last one was a real heart-tugger. The boy without a dad who brings Harley home and hides him from his mom—"

"Enough." The tone was razor-sharp.

Erin would have stopped anyway because of the "aha" moment. The light went on. "The little boy in all these stories is you."

"Right," he said sarcastically.

"I suggested you do stream-of-consciousness writing as a creative exercise and even told you it could be about Harley. You took my advice. This is what you've been working on so late every night."

"That's a stretch."

"I don't think so. It makes sense. The covert midnight sessions and your reaction right now prove I'm right. And you're acting as if I stole something from you."

"Your words."

"You're twisting them." Erin shook her head. "The thing is, you claimed not to be good at anything except being a soldier and it has to be said. You're wrong. I love these stories. And I love you."

Erin hadn't planned to say the last part but she'd never meant anything more. It was the honest truth. The only part she wished she could take back was Jack's reaction to hearing what was in her heart. It didn't seem possible, but he looked even more furious. Any second she expected his eyes to turn red and shoot fire.

He didn't move a muscle, until he did. Without warning, he crossed the space between them and took the file out of her hand. With a take-this look, he dropped it in the trash by the desk. "That's cleaning up."

"No, Jack. You need to send these to your agent. To Cheryl—"

He backed up several steps, as if he couldn't stand being so close to her. "I can't work with anyone I can't trust."

No, she thought. *I'm not ready to leave. Don't do it. Don't say it.* "Your editor hired me. You can't do this."

"Watch me." He moved to the door and opened it. "I'm taking my dog for a walk. Don't be here when I get back."

"No, Jack. Calm down—"

"Harley—"

For the first time Erin noticed the dog standing between them. He'd been so quiet and now she could see that the animal knew something was very wrong. He didn't react to the four-letter word that normally made him quiver with excitement. But after whining sadly and a last look at her, he followed Jack out the door.

Erin took the hesitation to mean the little guy cared about her and it was some comfort. Not much, but some.

She'd never been fired before. Certainly not by the man she was in love with. But he'd been quite clear and left her no choice. She was only here for the work and he refused to deal with her during the remainder of her contract. There was nothing left but for her to go.

The file in the trash caught her eye and she reached down to fish it out. She pressed the cardboard folder and its contents against her and whispered to the empty room, "No, Jack, that's cleaning up."

It didn't take Erin long to pack her things and load them in her rental car. She fought the urge to hang around until Jack returned from the walk, to try to change his mind. She didn't because he was in no mood to listen and, frankly, another rejection from him would destroy her.

So, with a heavy heart and a last look at the house and marina, she drove away from it and pulled out onto Lakeshore Drive. It must have been her state of shock, or muscle memory, but somehow she ended up in town. To get to the airport a hundred miles away, she needed to go through Blackwater Lake anyway.

The car needed gas and it wouldn't hurt to pick up a sandwich. The odds of her getting hungry any time in the foreseeable future were slim, what with a knot the size of a Toyota in her stomach. But she forced herself to be practical, even though every instinct she had was advising her to curl into the fetal position.

After filling up the gas tank she stopped at Bar None. It was sort of on the way out of town, at least that's what she told herself. The truth was darker and really more stupid than she'd have given herself credit for. Anyone here would know Jack because this was where he'd made his first friends. And she had an overwhelming need to unburden herself.

She went inside and hesitated, letting her eyes adjust to the dim interior. As it happened the place was empty, except for owner Delanie Carlson. She was standing behind the bar polishing glasses.

Erin walked over and sat on a stool. "Hi."

"Hey, yourself." The other woman looked at the door as if expecting it to open. "You alone?"

Completely, Erin thought, pain slicing through her. "Yes. I'd like to order a sandwich and cup of coffee. To go."

"You mean two, right?"

"No. Just the one." Only that morning she'd thought how lonely cooking for one was going to be, never thinking it would come so soon. Before she was prepared. "Turkey club, please."

"Okay." Delanie set the short glass down on the bar's scratched but gleaming surface. "What's Jack up to?"

"I don't know."

"Isn't it your job to watch him?" That was supposed to be funny.

"It was—" Erin blinked back the emotion that choked off her words.

"Was?" The other woman's blue eyes widened in surprise. "You're leaving?"

"Yes. I was always only temporary." Even though part of her had never abandoned hope that Jack might ask her to stay. What a fool she'd been.

"But this is…sudden."

Erin lifted one shoulder, putting all the nonchalance she could muster into the gesture. "If you have to go… Go."

"I can't believe Jack is letting you leave so easily."

There was a spurt of hope, which was dumb, but Erin couldn't help it. Any more than she could stop the question. "Why would you say that?"

"He was different with you. Lighter, somehow, if that makes any sense. Happy, and I think he hasn't been for a long time, if ever."

"That's nice of you to say." Erin had thought the same thing but found out the hard way how wrong she'd been. "But he doesn't need me."

"I'm not so sure." Delanie frowned.

"The book is nearly finished." *Along with several children's books that he threw in the trash. Idiot.* "My time is up a little early. So I'm heading back to Phoenix."

"Maybe you should stick around a couple days. Just in case he needs something."

"He won't." Not from her. She was untrustworthy.

When she got to the airport, she'd call Cheryl and report. The long drive would give her time to figure out how to explain her early exit. But that's not what was bothering her so much. The reality was that Jack handed back her heart because he didn't want it, or anything else from her. "I really need to get on the road so if I could just have my sandwich—"

Delanie hesitated as if she wanted to say more, then nodded. "Coming right up. And coffee."

"Yes."

The other woman turned away but not before the tears slid down Erin's cheeks. This was so much harder than she'd thought it would be. She was going to miss Blackwater Lake, the community spirit, the people.

Most of all she was going to miss Jack and was pretty sure she would forever.

Jack figured he had a couple more days to put in before the rough draft of his book would be finished. His editor should be happy he was working. After saving the new pages to the computer and a flash drive, he stretched then stood up. It was past dinnertime and he was hungry. The way Harley was looking at him meant the dog was hungry, too.

"Let's go, bud."

He grinned when the little guy raced over to the door. After *walk*, *go* was the word that made Harley quiver with anticipation. Jack, on the other hand, wasn't quivering with anything these days. Erin had been gone a week but he refused to believe he was doing anything but just fine on his own.

He opened the office door and Harley bounded down the stairs, then waited patiently on the front porch for Jack to let him inside. While he flipped on the lights, the dog ran down the hall into every room, as if searching for something. Moments later he came back and gave Jack the where-the-heck-is-she? look.

"Phoenix. Unless Corinne Carlisle needs a nosey book coach."

Jack listened to the sound of silence, the same sound he'd heard for the last seven days. No rattling pans in the kitchen. No closing cupboard doors. No amateur, ladylike swearing over lumpy gravy. If he didn't have Harley he would be talking to himself. The funny thing was that before Erin he hadn't minded that. Never gave a thought to the weirdness of talking only to his dog for long stretches of time. The fact that he thought about it now was annoying.

"Damn it." Harley trotted over as if to ask what was wrong. Jack dropped to one knee and rubbed his furry head. "She ruined the isolation for me."

And that wasn't all. She'd gone through his personal things. More unforgivable was the fact that she'd been right. She figured out that the lonely little boy in the Harley books was him. She'd looked inside him without permission and he couldn't stand the pity he saw in her eyes. Now he would never have to see it again because he'd never see *her* again.

That thought didn't make him feel as satisfied as he wanted to.

Jack opened the refrigerator and checked out its contents. There were multiple leftover containers where alien life forms were growing. This was the last of what she'd cooked for him. He shut the door with a little more force than was necessary.

"A beer and a burger," he said to no one in particular.

Jack put out Harley's food and made sure his water dish was full, then grabbed his keys from a hook on the wall. He felt a little guilty when the dog followed him to the front door. "Don't be inviting your friends over to party, bud."

It was cold outside but somehow it penetrated in a way he'd never noticed before. Just his imagination, he thought, as he walked to where the jeep was parked. The empty space beside it seemed to mock him. How stupid was that? He'd spent a lifetime being a loner and a couple months with a mouthy substitute teacher who got in his face all the time wasn't going to change that.

He would be fine. In a day or two.

Jack drove to Blackwater Lake and followed Main Street to Bar None. He pulled into the parking lot, which had quite a few cars for a weeknight. After settling in a space he exited the car and walked toward the building, with its neon flashing beer bottle in the window. On a sign over the roof proclaiming the name of the establishment there were crossed cocktail glasses.

When he walked inside people sitting in booths and the scattered tables looked up. A couple of them lifted a hand in greeting. That was different.

He recognized Kim Miller and her husband, Luke, teachers at the high school where he'd talked to the kids. April Kennedy sat at a table with Sheriff Will Fletcher. His bar buddy was part of a couple so Jack would have to go solo. That was okay. He was dusting off his loner cred anyway.

He sat on a stool at the bar, the one farthest away from anyone. Delanie Carlson was drawing a beer from the tap and gave him a nod, letting him know she would be right with him. Communicating without words, what a concept. And a welcome change.

After setting the glass in front of a cowboy, the red-headed bar owner walked over to him. "Hey, stranger."

"Hi."

"What can I get you?"

"Beer and burger," he said.

"Coming right up."

After drawing another beer, she set it on a cocktail napkin in front of him. She didn't ask how he liked his burger or if he wanted cheese because she already knew. There was something to be said for no surprises. He liked that.

While waiting for his order, Jack sipped on his drink and looked around the dimly lit interior. He recognized the checker from the grocery store, the one he'd never engaged in conversation until shopping with Erin. The mayor and her husband, who owned McKnight's Automotive, where the jeep got serviced, were sitting at a table with his daughter, Sydney, and her fiancé, Burke Holden.

Before Erin he'd been able to come in here and ignore everyone else. Now he couldn't.

Delanie walked over with a plate containing his food and set it in front of him. "Here you go."

"Thanks."

Instead of moving away, she rested her forearms on the bar, as if settling in for a chat. He hated to admit it but he craved a little company. Nothing heavy, just shallow small talk.

"How's business?"

"Good. Look at you initiating conversation." She smiled as if he was the star pupil.

"I've got skills." He ate a couple of fries.

"Maybe. But not so much with people." Her blue eyes narrowed. "Until Erin."

He grabbed a few more fries, intending to stuff them into his mouth, but stopped halfway there. Hearing someone say her name out loud was an awful lot like a sucker punch.

He didn't want to talk about her. "What's new?"

"Same old, same old." Delanie picked up a cloth and used it to wipe nonexistent spots off the shiny wooden surface of the bar. "So the rumor is that she left town earlier than expected."

Jack knew the "she" in question was Erin and figured the bar owner didn't share his inclination to avoid the subject. He put down the fries and took a drink of beer.

After a sip, he set it on the cocktail napkin and said, "It was time for her to go."

"Really? Are you sure about that?"

"Why wouldn't I be?"

"Oh, I don't know. Maybe because you look kind of lost. A little miserable. I'd have to say lonely."

"Looks can be deceiving," he retorted.

"For the average person. But I'm not easily fooled." She didn't bat an eye at the irritation in his voice. "People are my business. I listen, watch and talk to them every day. I've pretty much seen and heard it all, every story. Breakup, fight and lies. Even when someone is lying to themselves I can spot it a mile away. One look is worth a thousand words."

"I thought that was a picture."

"Whatever." She lifted one shoulder. "The point is I can see right through you. So why don't you tell me the real reason she left."

"Even if I do, how can you trust it? I make stuff up for a living," he warned.

"Didn't I just get finished explaining that I can spot a lie in a lineup?"

"Isn't there someone in this place who needs a refill?" Please, God.

"Touchy, aren't you?" Delanie looked around and seemed satisfied that everyone was happy. "And that was an attempt to distract me. Good try, but not good enough. Tell me why she left."

Jack thought about walking away and a couple of months ago he would have. But not now. And he refused to add "since Erin." "She went through my files."

"You mean writing files?"

"Yeah."

"The ones where you put things about making stuff up?" There was a hint of sarcasm in her voice.

"It's the principle." When he said it out loud his reasoning seemed trivial, inconsequential.

"So you let her go."

Jack wondered at the phrasing. She could have said he fired or terminated her, but didn't. "He let her go" put a very personal spin on what happened.

"She was leaving anyway."

"That's what she said."

"You saw her?" Jack shouldn't have been surprised but he was.

"Just before she left," Delanie confirmed. Her expression turned accusing. "You made her cry."

That one stuck. But he wouldn't let her know. "How can you be so sure it was about me?"

"Oh, please, Jack. Anyone with a brain could see how she felt about you. And you were a son of a bitch to her."

"She was leaving anyway. Sooner was better than later," he said again.

"Was she?" Delanie let the question hang there.

"Yes. She has a life somewhere else. Blackwater Lake was just a pit stop."

"Know what I think?"

"I have a feeling you're going to tell me," he said.

She grinned. "I think you found an excuse to be mad at her."

"Why would I do that?"

"So you could hide behind your self-righteous indignation. That way it wouldn't hurt when she was gone."

That hit closer to the target than he wanted to admit. But not hitting the bull's-eye qualified as a near miss. Which made her attempt off-the-mark. "You couldn't be more wrong."

"Has anyone ever told you that when you bury your head in the sand you leave your backside exposed?"

"Yes."

"And you don't think that's what you're doing?" she persisted.

"No."

"Then you're a jack-ass. No pun intended, Jack."

He'd abandoned being a loner to come here and be insulted? Didn't matter how close to the truth she was. He drank the last of his beer. "On second thought, can I get this burger to go?"

"Sure thing. I'll take care of it." Just before she turned away there was a look on her face that said her work there was done.

A minute or two later she came back with a to-go container for his uneaten food. "Take care, Jack."

"Yeah." Next time he wouldn't turn his back on this woman.

He'd thought a beer and a little trivial conversation would help, but that was his mistake. Another in a growing list.

He drove home and pulled into his space, with the empty one still there beside it. After grabbing his cold, crappy burger in a box, he got out and walked toward the porch. Again he had the sensation of being punched in the gut.

There were no welcoming lights or comfort-food dinners to look forward to. The scent of her skin was still there, but growing fainter every day. No one to plot his book with.

After having Erin, being alone sucked. And there was no hiding from it any longer.

Chapter Fifteen

Jack watched the digital clock on the microwave until it showed 9:05, then poured himself another cup of coffee and sat down at the kitchen table again. If Erin was here he would be late for the status meeting.

But Erin *wasn't* here.

He could do what he wanted to do when he wanted to do it. For the last two weeks he'd been doing just fine without her. The book was finished and he was reading it through one more time before sending the completed manuscript to his editor. He knew something was off, but couldn't quite put his finger on what was missing.

"Erin would know."

Jack didn't realize he'd said that out loud until Harley jumped up and looked hopeful before scurrying out of the room. The animal was going to find Erin, same as he had been for the last two weeks. Moments later the dog came back and stared at him as if to say "Do something to bring her back."

"I know you're missing her, buddy." He reached down and scratched the animal's head. "As much as I'm savoring my self-righteous indignation I understand where you're coming from. But work is waiting."

After grabbing his coffee mug, Jack headed for the front door and Harley trailed after him. He'd waited until after nine every morning for the last two weeks and felt a brief flash of anticipation before reality sank in again. There was no sunshine to look forward to. If she'd never been here he wouldn't know what he was missing.

He opened the office door and glanced around. Everything was just as he'd left it. Because no one was there to move stuff. Irritated, he set down his mug on his desk, right where the coffee stain was. No sissy coaster for him.

The printed-out manuscript was waiting for him and he sat down to finish editing. The action scenes were fine, the dialogue crisp, funny in the right places and moved the story forward. But every time Mac's assistant showed up on the page everything came to a grinding halt. And changing her name wouldn't solve the problem.

She was flat and one-dimensional. Mac's coffee was always waiting. She did exactly as told, never pushed back and was boring as hell. She didn't put pens and pencils in the mug where they belonged or put that coffee on the coaster he hated, or cook the best comfort food he'd ever tasted.

So there was something missing in his work, too. The female character Erin said this story needed wasn't her.

Jack remembered Delanie saying he'd found an excuse to be mad so it wouldn't hurt when Erin was gone. If she was right, the strategy was a complete failure because the pain tearing through him now hurt as surely as if someone put a bullet in him.

And he'd made her cry.

"I'm an idiot, Harley—" Without looking he reached

down, knowing the dog would be there. He rubbed his hand over the furry head and didn't feel the calm that usually settled over him. "A real bastard—"

The phone rang, startling him, and he looked at the caller ID. His editor. He picked up the receiver and hit the talk button. "Hi, Cheryl."

"Jack? Is that really you? Not a voice-mail message?"

"I deserve that."

"After avoiding me for months?" There was just a touch of sarcasm in her voice. "No. Don't beat yourself up. My feelings weren't hurt at all."

"Okay. Take your best shot. Get it out of your system."

"That's just mean. Giving me permission takes all the fun out of it." She laughed. "But I'll do my best. It wasn't hard at all to juggle the publishing schedule or put promotion on hold for you."

"I'm a son of a bitch." He'd just called himself worse and didn't blame this woman for dumping on him even more. "I guess you're wondering about the book. You should know—"

"I'll get to that, but there's something else I need to talk to you about."

Absently he rubbed Harley. "I get it. You're not finished chewing me out."

"No, I am. That's not it." There was a pause. "You've been holding out on me, Jack."

"I thought we already established I'm a jerk and my book is late."

"No. I meant the Harley books."

He went still. "The what?"

"The children's stories with the Chinese crested dog."

"Still don't know what you're talking about." He'd trashed the file.

"Erin sent me a folder with stories about a little boy who triumphs over adversity with the help of his dog."

Jack hadn't realized they were gone. The last time he'd seen them was when he took the file folder from Erin and threw it away. The bag of trash from his office went into the big container at the marina store, where it eventually was hauled off. And that was that. Or so he'd believed.

He waited for the anger to help him camouflage the pain but he was fresh out. That hadn't been the case when he found Erin reading his stuff. He could talk about it rationally because his editor was probably just trying to decide whether or not he had a screw loose.

"Those aren't really stories as much as creativity exercises. Just ignore them."

"Are you crazy?"

He hadn't thought so, but now he wasn't sure. "Why?"

"They're completely wonderful, Jack. Who'd have thought you, of all people, could write like this? With a message for children. Where did that come from?"

Erin knew, he thought. She'd figured out almost right away that the little boy in the stories was him. She saw into his soul and surely couldn't care about him after that. So he fired her. And made her cry.

He was a rat-bastard son of a bitch.

But Cheryl was waiting for an answer. "Like I said, it was something I did to get the writing motor started."

"It worked."

"What does that mean?" he asked.

"I sent the proposal over to the children's division and they love it."

"What?"

"I hope that was all right." She must have heard something in his voice because for the first time she sounded doubtful. "You did send them to be considered for publication, no?"

He hadn't sent them at all. It took someone who believed

in him to pass them along. Where was your self-righteous indignation when you really needed it?

"It's all right" was all he could think of to say.

"Good. Because there will be an offer coming. We'll contact your agent and he'll be in touch."

"You're serious about this? You really want to buy them?" That sounded an awful lot like "you really like me?" But he couldn't hold back the question.

"This is a new career direction. Just in case you decide to kill off Mac Daniels," she said. "A lot of well-known authors are branching into children's and young adult genres. I just never thought you would be one of them."

"Should I be insulted?" he asked.

"I can't stop you and it's not what I meant." She laughed. "It was a compliment. But, fair warning, we're going to want you to do some media."

Before he'd met Erin, he would have shut down the idea. But he'd done the interview for the Blackwater Lake newspaper and lived to talk about it. Logan had told him the issue with the article about their local author had set a record for newspaper sales. And he never would have agreed if Erin hadn't talked him into it. Since she showed up at his door life had done a one-eighty on him and nothing bad happened. If he didn't count her leaving.

"I'll do media," he said.

"Wow." There was stunned silence for a moment. "That's it. Just wow."

"Was that sarcastic?" he asked.

"Maybe a little." Again there was a pause before she said, "About the other book. The sequel to *High Value Target*…"

"It's finished."

"Great. I can't wait to read it," she said.

"About that—"

"Jack, you have to let it go sometime. No one likes a

clean, problem-free manuscript more than me, but I really need to see this book."

"Look—" He leaned back and stared at the empty chair in front of his desk, the one where Erin always sat. If she could hear what he was about to say there would be no living with her. Actually there was no living with her now. Self-righteous indignation completely deserted him and the dam on his pain crumbled, letting it all rush in. "The book needs a little tweaking. Not the story. It's fine. Just something isn't right."

"I don't know, Jack—"

"I know it's a lot to ask and I don't deserve it, but can you give me a couple of weeks for a small revision? I'll send you a detailed outline."

There was a long, tense silence before Cheryl sighed. "Okay. You've got two weeks. Max."

"Thanks. You're the best."

"Yes, I am. After all, I sent you Erin."

"You did."

That was a blessing and a curse. Living the blessing was the best time he'd ever had. The curse part he could do without and had no one but himself to blame.

"She really brought out your creativity, Jack. At the risk of patting myself on the back, I have to say that she's good for you."

If ripping a guy's heart out was the goal, then yeah, she was good for him. But that was information better kept to himself, so he did.

"So what did you do to her?"

The question came out of left field and caught him off guard. Somewhere this professional conversation had taken a personal turn. "I'm not sure what you're asking."

"I don't think that's true. But you're a man so I'll explain. Erin is different since she spent time with you. I sent you an outgoing, cheerful young woman to help with your manuscript and she came back distant and, there's no other way to say it...she's sad."

Jack drew in a breath. He was a writer. Words were his weapon of choice. But he couldn't think of anything bad enough to call himself for what he'd done. And apparently she hadn't told Cheryl about being fired or his editor would have mentioned it.

"Jack? You didn't hang up on me, did you?"

"Still here," he answered.

"I'll say it straight out. I'd like to know what happened because you broke my book coach."

From his point of view she'd broken him. When Erin arrived he'd been a fat, dumb and happy loner. Now he was talking to his dog about plot twists. But this woman deserved something. "What happened is that she brought out more than just my creativity."

"You fell in love with her." Cheryl wasn't asking a question.

And he wasn't going to tell her she was right. His editor shouldn't be the first one to hear the truth.

"I'm sorry for the delay on this book. I apologize for any inconvenience to you and the publisher. It will never happen again. You'll have it in two weeks. I give you my word on that."

"Okay, Jack."

After saying goodbye he hung up. There was a manuscript to deal with, then the real work would start.

He'd made Erin cry and somehow he had to fix that.

Erin sat behind the desk in front of the classroom and monitored the seniors who were taking a pop quiz. They didn't know it wouldn't count toward their grade and was basically busywork. In about fifteen minutes the final bell of the day would ring and she could go home and curl into a protective ball. It had been her go-to coping mechanism since Jack threw her out a month ago.

How long would she feel so empty inside? she wondered, because this funk showed no sign of letting up anytime soon.

The flip side of the final bell was that she'd have to assume her coping mechanism in her lonely apartment. Maybe she should stop at the dog-rescue shelter again and get a pet for companionship. She'd really become attached to Harley. And Jack... Her eyes filled at the thought of him but crying in front of a room full of teenagers wasn't an option. Darn it, why did she have to go and fall in love with him?

She looked at the clock again. "Okay, class. Time is up."

There was a collective groan and automatic protests of not being finished with the test they'd griped about taking in the first place.

"Mrs. Castillo warned you she would do this and instructed me to be firm." She stood. "Please pass your papers forward."

The sound of paper shuffling filled the room and her back was turned, which was why she didn't hear the door opening or see who walked in.

"Who's the dude with the weird-looking dog?" one of the students asked.

Erin whirled around and saw Jack just inside the door with Harley in his arms. After one bark, the little guy wiggled until Jack set him down. His paws had barely hit the ground before he ran to her.

She dropped to one knee and took his noble little face in her hands, scratching him under his chin. "Hi, Harley. You're such a handsome dog. I've missed you."

"Miss Riley? Should we notify the office?" one of the guys asked.

"It's okay," Jack said. "I stopped to see the principal and for probably the first time I wasn't even in trouble."

The kids laughed at his joke and it would have been funny to her under different circumstances.

"I know him," Erin said. "This is Jack Garner, the author of the runaway bestselling book *High Value Target*."

"Why did Mr. Pascale let you in with the dog?" a girl asked.

"I vouched for him," Jack explained. "I have permission just this once. And if anyone asks, he's a service dog."

"I know him, too," Erin said. "His name is Harley."

"My dad read your book." The girl in the first desk couldn't take her eyes off the author.

Erin knew the feeling, but she was in charge here and it was time to take control of the class, at least, even if she was having trouble managing her feelings. She couldn't look at Jack hard enough and her heart was racing, trying to outrun the pain of seeing him again.

She ignored both and took the quiz papers that were passed to her, noting that the bell would ring in a few minutes. She'd make her escape then. "Never miss a teachable moment. Jack, why don't you tell the kids about yourself."

"Just the high points? Maybe five minutes?"

"Yes." That was the advice she'd given him when he'd shown up at Kim Miller's classroom in Blackwater Lake without notes for his talk. He'd remembered and she found that oddly endearing. Foolish, but true.

So, Jack told his personal story again and, like the last time, didn't gloss over the fact that he'd chosen the army over juvenile detention and liked the life so much he joined the rangers. But for every up there was a down. He lost brothers in arms that he cared deeply about and it left a mark. Writing helped him deal with those scars and he got lucky.

Then he asked if anyone had a question and most of the hands in the room shot up. He pointed to a kid sitting in the middle row.

"What's your name?" Jack asked.

"Cameron. How do you know Miss Riley?"

Jack met her gaze. "I was having trouble with my second book. My editor sent her to me to move things along. I'd never collaborated before and it didn't go well at first."

Because he was a loner, she thought. She wasn't sure what he was doing here, but there was no reason to think he'd changed. She watched him answer the kids' questions in a straightforward, humorous way and he had them firmly under his spell. So what else was new?

She recalled the moments before his first time in front of a high school class, when he'd said it was too late for a personality transplant and no one had ever accused him of being charming or approachable. Apparently he was capable of learning because he was both of those things now.

Good God, would the darn bell ever ring?

A girl in front of him asked, "You said you live in Montana. Why did you come all this way to see Miss Riley?"

He looked over at her, but before he could answer the question, the darn bell finally rang. She really wanted to know why he'd come, but this group didn't need to hear the free-at-last signal twice. They grabbed their things and headed for the door.

Jack called after them, "Thanks for not throwing spitballs at me."

And suddenly it was quiet. She was alone with Jack.

Erin moved to the desk and retrieved her purse from the bottom drawer. "That's my cue. I'll just be going—"

"Please wait."

She looked down for a moment, then slid her hands into the pockets of her black slacks. With a deep breath she forced herself to meet his gaze. "I don't think we have anything to say to each other. You made yourself clear the last time I saw you."

"You're not at all curious about why I'm here?"

She was trying not to be and failing miserably. "Okay. Yes. Why are you here?"

He watched his dog wander the classroom, exploring and stopping occasionally to sniff something that caught his attention. "I know you sent the Harley books to Cheryl."

"So you came all this way to yell at me for violating your privacy? News flash, Jack, you can only fire me once. After that, technically I don't work for you anymore and it's—"

He moved closer and touched a finger to her lips, stopping the flow of words. "She loved the stories."

"What?"

"Cheryl passed them on to the editor in charge of children's books and they bought them. Everyone at the house loves the idea of an ongoing series."

"Congratulations." Oh, she wanted to rub that in, but taking the high road seemed... The hell with the high road. She'd already been fired. There was nothing left to lose. "I told you so."

"What?"

"I knew they were good but you wouldn't listen."

He nodded. "I was an ungrateful jerk."

"Yes, you were." There. She'd said it and waited to feel some satisfaction. Unfortunately, there was nothing.

"I came here to explain why I reacted so badly."

"It's not necessary. I get it. You felt vulnerable revealing so much of yourself."

"It's more than that." The easy charm he showed the

kids was gone, replaced by a tightly coiled intensity. The warrior. He was fighting for something. "I believed when you saw the real me you'd be disappointed and—"

"Leave?"

"Yeah." He folded his arms over his chest. "Sending you away first was my way to control the situation. It was knee-jerk."

Gosh darn it, she understood and didn't want to. She was trying to stay mad at him because it was the only protection she had.

"You really didn't have to come, Jack."

"Yeah, I did. Cheryl said I broke her book coach."

"What?" Erin never mentioned what had happened between her and Jack. How could the editor have known?

"She said you were different. Sad." He looked troubled for a moment, then went on. "Delanie said you stopped by on the way out of town and you were crying."

"She was wrong." Talk about knee-jerk. "Bar None is dark. I had something in my eye."

"Liar."

She had seen many expressions cross his face. Anger. Irritation. Passion. Intensity. Tenderness and toughness. But there was a look now that was different from anything else. It had all the signs of self-recrimination. "Okay. I may have shed a tear. But it had nothing to do with you." Now *that* was a lie. "I've never been fired before. It was a shock."

"I'm sorry I made you cry, Erin. It was definitely not my finest hour."

"Understood. But it wasn't necessary to come all this way to apologize. Although I appreciate it and accept your apology. Now I really need to go." She started to reach for her purse again. "We're done."

"I'm not."

"What else could there possibly be?" She wasn't sure how much longer she could keep it together and wished he would leave.

"You never asked about the sequel to *High Value Target*." He held up his hand to stop her when she started to say something. "I thought you should know that I figured out what was missing from the book. And from my life."

"What?" She held her breath as hope twisted free inside her.

"The answer to both is you. I love you, Erin."

She had an imagination and knew how to use it. She'd pictured a scenario where Jack would say those words to her. Never once had she seen herself bursting into tears, but that's what happened. The feelings came spilling out and she covered her face with her hands.

Instantly, strong arms pulled her in close to his body. "Please don't cry. I can't stand it."

She laughed, but it came out more a snort. "You? Big, bad Special Forces ranger?"

"It's our secret. I'd rather face incoming fire than see you cry." He cupped her cheek in his palm and lifted her gaze to his. "I love you. I came to get you and bring you home to Blackwater Lake. I'm asking you to marry me. If you meant what you said. That you love me."

She sniffled, then pulled away just far enough to look into his eyes. "Yes."

He waited, looking increasingly frustrated. Finally he said, "That's all you've got? I expected more."

"Show, don't tell." She shrugged, then stood on tiptoe and pressed her mouth to his. She poured all the pain of rejection and now unexpected joy into the kiss. Both of them had trouble catching their breath when they reluctantly pulled apart.

"Sometimes a guy needs more than a word. Does that mean you'll marry me?"

"I love you, Jack. No one warned me you would be so much trouble, but I fell in love with you the moment we met."

"Love at first sight?"

"Laugh if you want, but it's true."

"I'm not laughing. Thanks to you my career in action-adventure is on target and I'm doing a series of children's books." He lifted one shoulder. "Even I couldn't have made this up. So, who knows? Maybe together we'll break into the romance genre."

"The best part is we'll live it. Nothing would make me happier than marrying you. And I love Blackwater Lake, too. Just try and keep me away." She smiled up at him. "Is that enough words for you?"

"For now. But there's a lot to be said for 'show, don't tell.'"

And he proceeded to kiss her again. Being in his arms was like coming home. Life was funny and wonderful. She'd taken a job looking for adventure and found the most exciting one of all. Love.

A word with the bachelor had turned into her happily-ever-after.

* * * * *

Can't get enough of
THE BACHELORS OF BLACKWATER LAKE?
Don't miss Teresa Southwick's previous books in this heartwarming miniseries:

HOW TO LAND HER LAWMAN
THE WIDOW'S BACHELOR BARGAIN
A DECENT PROPASAL
THE RANCHER WHO TOOK HER IN

Drake Carson is willing to put up with Luce Hale, the supposed "expert" his mother brought to the ranch, as long as she can get the herd of wild horses off his land, but the pretty academic wants to study them instead! Sparks are sure to fly when opposites collide in Mustang Creek...

Read on for a sneak peek from New York Times *bestselling author Linda Lael Miller's second book in* THE CARSONS OF MUSTANG CREEK *trilogy,* ALWAYS A COWBOY, *coming September 2016 from HQN Books.*

CHAPTER ONE

THE WEATHER JUST plain sucked, but that was okay with Drake Carson. In his opinion, rain was better than snow any day of the week, and as for sleet… Well, that was wicked, especially in the wide-open spaces, coming at a person in stinging blasts like a barrage of buckshot. Yep, give him a slow, gentle rainfall every time, the kind that generally meant spring was in the works. Anyhow, he could stand to get a little wet. Here in Wyoming, this close to the mountains, the month of May might bring sunshine and pastures blanketed with wildflowers, but it could also mean a rogue snowstorm fit to bury folks and critters alike.

Raising his coat collar around his ears, he nudged his horse into motion with his heels. Starburst obeyed, although he seemed hesitant about it, even edgy, and Drake wondered why. For almost a year now, livestock had gone missing—mostly calves, but the occasional steer or heifer, too. While it didn't happen often, for a rancher, a single lost animal was one too many. The spread was big, and he couldn't keep an eye on the whole place at once, of course.

He sure as hell tried, though.

"Stay with me," he told his dogs, Harold and Violet, a pair of German shepherds from the same litter and some of the best friends he'd ever had.

Then, tightening the reins slightly, in case Starburst took a notion to bolt out of his easy trot, he looked around, narrowing his eyes to see through the downpour. Whatever he'd expected to spot—a grizzly or a wildcat or a band of modern-day rustlers, maybe—he *hadn't* expected a lone female just up ahead, crouched behind a small tree and clearly drenched, despite the dark rain slicker covering her slender form.

She was peering through a pair of binoculars, having taken no apparent notice of Drake, his dogs or his horse. Even with the rain pounding down, they should have been hard to miss, being only fifty yards away.

Whoever this woman might be, she wasn't a neighbor or a local, either. Drake would have recognized her if she'd lived in or around Mustang Creek, and the whole ranch was posted against trespassers, mainly to keep tourists out. A lot of visiting sightseers had seen a few too many G-rated animal movies, and thought they could cozy up to a bear, a bison or a wolf for a selfie to post on social media.

Most times, if the damn fools managed to get away alive, they were missing a few body parts or the family pet.

Drake shook off the images and concentrated on the subject at hand—the woman in the rain slicker.

Who was she, and what was she doing on Carson property?

A stranger, yes.

But it dawned on Drake that, whatever else she might be, she *wasn't* the reason his big Appaloosa was suddenly so skittish.

The woman was fixated on the wide meadow, actually a shallow valley, just beyond the copse of cottonwood, and so, Drake realized now, was Starburst.

He stood in his stirrups and squinted, and his heart picked up speed as he caught sight—finally—of the band of wild mustangs grazing there. Once numbering only half a dozen or so, the herd had grown to more than twenty.

Now, alerted by the stallion, their leader and the unqualified bane of Drake's existence, they scattered.

He was vigilant, that devil on four feet, and cocky, too.

He lingered for a few moments, while the mares fled in the opposite direction, tossed his magnificent head and snorted.

Too late, sucker.

Drake cursed under his breath and promptly forgot all about the woman who shouldn't have been there in the first damn place, his mind on the expensive mare—make that *mares*—the stallion had stolen from him. He whistled through his teeth, the piercing whistle that brought tame horses running, ready for hay, a little sweet feed and a warm stall.

He hadn't managed to get this close to the stallion and his growing harem in a long while, and he hated to let the opportunity pass, but he knew that if he gave chase, the dogs would be right there with him, and probably wind up getting their heads kicked in.

The stallion whinnied, taunting him, and sped away, topping the rise on the other side of the meadow and vanishing with the rest.

The dogs whimpered, itching to run after them, but Drake ordered them to stay; then he whipped off his hat, rain be damned, and smacked it hard against his thigh in pure exasperation. This time, he cussed in earnest.

Harold and Violet were fast and they were agile, but he'd raised them from pups and he couldn't risk letting them get hurt.

Hope stirred briefly when Drake's prize chestnut quarter horse, a two-year-old mare destined for greatness, reappeared at the crest of the hill opposite, ears pricked at the familiar whistle, but the stallion came back for her, crowding her, nipping at her neck and flanks, and then she was gone again.

Damn it all to hell.

"Thanks for nothing, mister."

It was the intruder, the trespasser. The woman stormed toward Drake through the rain-bent grass, waving the binoculars like a maestro raising a baton at the symphony. If he hadn't been so annoyed by her mere presence, let alone her nerve—yelling at him like that when *she* was the one in the wrong—he might have been amused.

She was a sight for sure, plowing through the grass, all fuss and fury and wet to the skin.

Mildly curious now that the rush of adrenaline roused by losing another round to that son-of-a-bitching stallion was beginning to subside, Drake waited with what was, for him, uncommon patience. He hoped the approaching tornado, pint-size but definitely category five, wouldn't step on a snake before she completed the charge.

Born and raised on this land, he wouldn't have stomped around like that, not without keeping a close eye out for rattlers.

As she got closer, he made out an oval face, framed by the hood of her coat, and a pair of amber eyes that flashed as she demanded, "Do you have any idea how long it took me to get that close to those horses? Days! And what happens? *You* have to come along and ruin everything!"

Drake resettled his hat, tugging hard at the brim, and waited.

The woman all but stamped her feet. "Days!" she repeated wildly.

Drake felt his mouth twitch. "Excuse me, ma'am, I'm a bit confused. You're here because…?"

"Because of the horses!" The tone and pitch of her voice said he was an idiot for even asking. Apparently he ought to be able to read her mind instead.

He gave himself points for politeness—and for managing a reasonable tone. "I see," he said, although of course he didn't.

"The least you could do is apologize," she informed him, glaring.

Still mounted, Drake adjusted his hat again. The dogs sat on either side of him and Starburst, staring at the woman as if she'd sprung up out of the ground.

When he replied, he sounded downright amiable. In his own opinion, anyway. "Apologize? Now, why would I do that? Given that I *live* here, I mean. This is private property, Ms.—"

She wasn't at all fazed to find out that she was on somebody else's land, uninvited. Nor did she offer her name.

"It took me hours to track those horses down," she ranted on, still acting like the offended party, "in this weather, no less! I finally get close enough, and you—you..." She paused, but only to suck in a breath so she could go right on strafing him with words. "*You* try hiding behind a tree without moving a muscle, waiting practically forever, and with water dripping down your neck."

He might have pointed out that he was no stranger to inclement weather, since he rode fence lines in blizzards and rounded up strays under a hot sun—and those were the *easy* days—but he refrained. "What were you doing there, behind my tree?"

"*Your* tree? No one owns a tree."

"Maybe not, but people can own the ground it grows on. And that's the case here, I'm afraid."

She rolled her eyes.

Great, a tree hugger. She probably drove one of those little hybrid cars, plastered with bumper stickers, and cruised along at thirty miles an hour in the left lane.

Nobody loved nature more than he did, but hell, the Carsons had held the deed to this ranch for more than a century, and it wasn't a public campground with hiking trails, nor was it a state park.

Drake leaned forward in the saddle. "Do the words *no trespassing* mean anything to you?" he asked sternly.

On some level, though, he was enjoying this encounter way more than he should have.

She merely glowered up at him, arms folded, chin raised.

He sighed. "All right. Let's see if we can clarify matters. That tree—" he gestured to the one she'd taken refuge behind earlier, and spoke very slowly so she'd catch his drift "—is on land my family owns. I'm Drake Carson. And you are?"

The look of surprise on her face was gratifying. "*You're* Drake Carson?"

"I was when I woke up this morning," he said in a deliberate drawl. "I don't imagine that's changed since then." A measured pause. "Now, how about answering my original question? What are you doing here?"

She seemed to wilt, and Drake supposed that was a victory, however small, but he wasn't inclined to celebrate. "I'm studying the horses."

The brim of his hat spilled water down his front as he nodded. "Well, yeah, I kind of figured that. It's really not the point, now, is it? Like I said, this is private property. And if you'd asked permission to be here, I'd know it."

She blushed, but no explanation was forthcoming. "So you're *him*."

"Yes, ma'am. You—"

The next moment, she was blustering again. "Tall man on a tall horse," she remarked, her tone scathing.

A few seconds earlier, he'd been in charge here. Now he felt defensive, which was ridiculous.

He drew a deep breath, released it slowly and spoke with quiet authority. He hoped. "My height and my horse have nothing to do with anything, as far as I can see. My point, once again, is you don't have the right to be here, much less yell at me."

"Yes, I do."

Of all the freaking gall. Drake glowered at the young woman standing next to his horse by then, unafraid, giving as good as she got. "What?"

"I *do* have the right to be here," she insisted. "I asked your mother's permission to come out and study the wild horses, and she said yes. In fact, she was very supportive."

Well, shit.

Would've been nice if his mother had bothered to mention it to him.

For some reason, he couldn't back off, or not completely, anyway. Call it male pride. "Okay," he said evenly. "*Why* do you want to study wild horses? Considering that they're...*wild* and everything."

She seemed thoroughly undaunted. "I'm doing my graduate thesis on how wild horses exist and interact with domesticated animals on working ranches." She added with emphasis, "And how ranchers deal with them. Like you."

So he was part of the equation. Yippee.

"Just so you understand," he said, "you aren't going to study *me*."

"What if I got your mother's permission?" she asked sweetly.

"Very funny." By then, Drake's mood was headed straight downhill. What was he doing out here in the damn rain, bantering with some self-proclaimed intellectual, when all he'd had before leaving the house this morning was a skimpy breakfast and one cup of coffee? The saddle leather creaked as he bent toward her. "Listen, Ms. Who-ever-you-are, I don't give a rat's ass about your thesis, or your theories about ranchers and wild horses, either. Do what you have to do, try not to get yourself killed and then move on to whatever's next on your agenda—preferably elsewhere."

Not surprisingly, the woman wasn't intimidated. "Hale," she announced brightly. "My name is Lucinda Hale, but everybody calls me Luce."

He inhaled, a long, deep breath. If he'd ever had that much trouble learning a woman's name before, he didn't recall the occasion. "Ms. Hale, then," he began, tugging at the brim of his hat in a gesture that was more automatic than cordial. "I'll leave you to it. While I'm sure your work is absolutely fascinating, I have plenty of my own to do. In short, while I've enjoyed shadowboxing with you, I'm fresh out of leisure time."

He might've been talking to a wall. "Oh, don't worry," she said cheerfully. "I wouldn't *dream* of interfering. I'll be an observer, that's all. Watching, figuring out how things work, making a few notes. You won't even know I'm around."

Drake sighed inwardly and reined his horse away, although he didn't use his heels. The dogs, still fascinated by the whole scenario, sat tight. "You're right, Ms. Hale. I won't know you're around, because you won't be. Around *me*, that is."

"You really are a very difficult man," she observed almost sadly. "Surely you can see the value of my project. Interactions between wild animals, domesticated ones and human beings?"

LUCE WAS COLD, wet, a little amused and *very* intrigued.

Drake Carson was gawking at her as though she'd just popped in from a neighboring dimension, wearing a tutu and waving a wand. His two beautiful dogs, waiting obediently for some signal from their master, seemed equally curious.

The consternation on his face was absolutely priceless.

And a very handsome face it was, at least what she could see of it in the shadow of his hat brim. If he had the same features as his younger brother Mace, whom she'd met earlier that day, he was one very good-looking man.

She decided to push him a bit further. "You run this ranch, don't you?"

"I do my best."

She liked his voice, which was calm and carried a low drawl. "Then you're the one I want."

Oh, no, she thought, that came out all wrong.

"For my project, I mean."

His strong jawline tightened visibly. "I don't have time to babysit you," he said. "This is a working ranch, not a resort."

"As I've said repeatedly, Mr. Carson, you won't have to do anything of the sort. I can take care of myself, and I'll stay out of your way as much as possible."

He seemed unconvinced. Even irritated.

But he didn't ride away.

Luce had already been warned that he wouldn't take to her project.

Talk about an understatement.

Mentally, she cataloged the things she'd learned about Drake Carson.

He was in charge of the ranch, which spanned thousands of acres and was home to lots of cattle and horses, as well as wildlife. The Carsons had very deep ties to Bliss County, Wyoming, going back several generations. He loved the outdoors, was good with animals, especially horses.

He was, in fact, a true cowboy.

He was also on the quiet side, solitary by nature, slow to anger—but watch out if he did. At thirty-two, Drake had never been married; he was college-educated, and once he'd gotten his degree, he'd come straight back to the ranch, having no desire to live anywhere else. He worked from sunrise to sunset and often longer.

Harry, the housekeeper whose real name was Harriet Armstrong, had dished up some sort of heavenly pie when Luce had arrived at the main ranch house, fairly early in the day. As soon as she understood who Luce was and why she was there, she'd proceeded to spill information about Drake at a steady clip.

Luce had encountered Mace Carson, Drake's younger brother, very briefly, when he'd come in from the family vineyard expressly for a piece of pie. Harry had introduced them and explained Luce's mission—i.e., to gather material for her thesis and interview Drake in depth, and get the rancher's perspective.

Mace had smiled slightly and shaken his head in response. "I'm glad you're here, Ms. Hale, but I'm afraid my brother isn't going to be a whole lot of use as a research subject. He's into his work and not much else, and he doesn't like to be distracted from it. Makes him testy."

A quick glance in Harry's direction had confirmed the sinking sensation created by Mace's words. The other woman had given a small, reluctant nod of agreement.

Well, Luce thought now, standing face-to-horse with Drake, they'd certainly known what they were talking about.

Drake was *definitely* testy.

He stared grimly into the rainy distance for a long moment, then muttered, "As if that damn stallion wasn't enough to get under my skin—"

"Cheer up," Luce said. She loved a challenge. "I'm here to help."

Drake gave her a long, level look. "Why didn't you say so in the first place?" he drawled, without a hint of humor. He flung out his free hand for emphasis, the reins resting easily in the other one. "My problems are over."

"Didn't you tell me you were leaving?" Luce asked.

He opened his mouth, closed it again, evidently reconsidering whatever he'd been about to say. Finally, with a mildly defensive note in his voice, he went on. "I planned to," he said, "but if I did, you'd be out here alone." He looked around. "Where's your horse? You won't be getting close to those critters again today. The stallion will see to that."

Luce's interest was genuine. "You sound as if you know him pretty well."

"We understand each other, all right," Drake said. "We should. We've been playing this game for a couple of years now."

That tidbit was going in her notes.

She shook her head in belated answer to his question about her means of transportation. "I don't have a horse," she explained. "I parked on a side road and hiked out here."

The day had been breathtakingly beautiful, before the clouds lowered and thickened and dumped rain. She'd hiked in all the western states and in Europe, and this was some gorgeous country. The Grand Tetons were just that. Grand.

"The nearest road is miles from here. You came all this way *on foot*?" Drake frowned at her. "Did my mother know you were crazy when she agreed to let you do your study here?"

"I actually enjoy hiking. A little rain doesn't bother me. I'll dry off back at the ranch."

"Back at the ranch?" he repeated slowly. Warily.

This was where she could tell him that his mother and hers were old friends, but she chose not to do it. She didn't want to take advantage of that relationship—or at least *appear* to be taking advantage of it. "That's a beautiful house you live in, by the way. Not what I expected to find on a place like this—chandeliers and oil paintings and wainscoting and all. Hardly the Ponderosa." She beamed a smile at Drake. "I was planning to camp out, but your mother generously invited me to stay on the ranch. My room has a wonderful view of the mountains. It's going to be glorious, waking up to that every morning."

Drake, she soon discovered, was still a few beats behind. "You're *staying* with us?"

"How else can I observe you in your native habitat?" Luce offered up another smile, her most innocent one. The truth was, she intended to camp some of the time, if only to avoid the long walk from the house. One of the main reasons she'd chosen this specific project was Drake himself, although she certainly wasn't going to tell him that! She'd known, even before Harry filled her in on the more personal aspects of his life, that he was an animal advocate, as well as a prominent rancher, that he had a degree in ecology. She'd first seen his name in print when she was still an undergrad, just a quote in an article, expressing his belief that running a large cattle operation could be done without endangering wildlife or the environment. Knowing that her mother and Blythe Carson were close had been a deciding factor, too, of course—a way of gaining access.

She allowed herself a few minutes to study the man. He sat on his horse confidently relaxed and comfortable in the saddle, the reins loosely held. The well-trained animal stood there calmly, clipping grass but not moving otherwise during their discussion.

Drake broke into her reverie by saying, "Guess I'd better take you back before something happens to you." He leaned toward her, reaching down. "Climb on."

She looked at the proffered hand and bit her lip, hesitant to explain that she'd ridden only once—an ancient horse at summer camp when she was twelve, and she'd been terrified the whole time.

No, she couldn't tell him that. Her pride wouldn't let her.

Besides, she wouldn't be steering the huge gelding; Drake would. And there was no denying the difficulties the weather presented.

She'd gotten some great footage during the afternoon and made a few notes, which meant the day wasn't a total loss.

"My backpack's heavy," she pointed out, her brief courage faltering. The top of that horse was pretty far off the ground. She could climb mountains, for Pete's sake, but that was different; she'd been standing on her own two feet the whole time.

At last, Drake smiled, and the impact of that smile was palpable. He was still leaning toward her, still holding out his hand. "Starburst's knees won't buckle under the weight of a backpack," he told her. "Or your weight, either."

The logic was irrefutable.

Drake slipped his booted foot out from the stirrup to make room for hers. "Come on. I'll haul you up behind me."

She handed up the backpack, sighed heavily. "Okay," she said. Then, gamely, she took Drake's hand. His grip was strong, and he swung her up behind him with no apparent effort.

It was easy to imagine this man working with horses and digging postholes for fences.

Settled on the animal's broad back, Luce had no choice

but to put her arms around his lean waist and hang on. For dear life.

The rain was coming down harder, and conversation was impossible.

Gradually, Luce relaxed enough to loosen her grip on Drake's middle.

A little, anyway.

Now that she was fairly sure she wasn't facing certain death, Luce allowed herself to enjoy the ride. Intrepid hiker though she was, the thought of trudging back to her car in a driving rain made her wince.

She hadn't missed the irony of the situation, either. She wanted to study wild horses, but she didn't know how to ride a tame one. Drake would be well within his rights to point that out to her, although she sensed, somehow, that he wouldn't.

When they finally reached the ranch house, he was considerate enough not to laugh when she slid clumsily off the horse and almost landed on her rear in a giant puddle. No, he simply tugged at the brim of his hat, suppressing a smile, and rode away without looking back.

Don't miss
ALWAYS A COWBOY
by New York Times *bestselling author*
Linda Lael Miller, available wherever HQN books
and ebooks are sold.

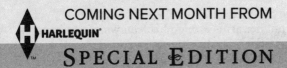
Available September 20, 2016

#2503 MS. BRAVO AND THE BOSS
The Bravos of Justice Creek • by Christine Rimmer
Jed Walsh has finally found the perfect assistant to put up with his extreme writing process in a down-on-her-luck caterer named Elise Bravo. He refuses to give in to their attraction and vows to make her stay on as his assistant, but he never thought she'd be able to lay claim to the heart he didn't even know he had.

#2504 MAVERICK VS. MAVERICK
Montana Mavericks: The Baby Bonanza • by Shirley Jump
Lindsay Dalton is drawn to Walker Jones III from the first time she sees him. The only problem? Their first meeting is in a courthouse—and she's suing him! Walker has met his match in Lindsay, but when they are forced to work together, they might just have more in common than they ever expected.

#2505 ROPING IN THE COWGIRL
Rocking Chair Rodeo • by Judy Duarte
Shannon Cramer is a nurse at the Rocking Chair Rodeo, a retirement home for cowboys. When she and Blake Darnell, a headstrong attorney, butt heads over a May-December romance between his uncle and her aunt, they're surprised to encounter sparks of desire and a romance of their own.

#2506 BUILDING THE PERFECT DADDY
Those Engaging Garretts! • by Brenda Harlen
Lauryn Garrett has no intention of falling for the sexy handyman in charge of her home renovations, but Ryder Wallace knows how to fix all kinds of things—even a single mother's broken heart. As eager as Ryder is to get his hands on Lauryn's house, it is the wounded woman who lives there who can teach him a thing or two about building a family.

#2507 THE MAN SHE SHOULD HAVE MARRIED
The Crandall Lake Chronicles • by Patricia Kay
Olivia Britton may be developing feelings for Matt Britton, her dead husband's brother, but her mother is trying to have her declared an unfit mother to little Thea, the daughter her husband never got to meet. Matt's been in love with Olivia for years and he's not going to let his mother's prejudice get in their way. Can they overcome a bitter mother-in-law and a lawsuit to create the family they've always dreamed of?

#2508 A WEDDING WORTH WAITING FOR
Proposals in Paradise • by Katie Meyer
Samantha Farley is back in Paradise, Florida, once again trying to fit in and make friends, now with the added pressure of her job riding on the outcome. Dylan Turner offers to use his status as town heartthrob to boost her social profile, secretly hoping to convince her they'd be perfect together. Will they be able to handle town gossip and past heartbreaks to find their way to happily-ever-after?

YOU CAN FIND MORE INFORMATION ON UPCOMING HARLEQUIN® TITLES, FREE EXCERPTS AND MORE AT WWW.HARLEQUIN.COM.

HSECNM0916

SPECIAL EXCERPT FROM

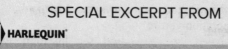

HARLEQUIN

SPECIAL EDITION

*Walker Jones III and Lindsay Dalton go head-to-head
in a lawsuit, but their legal maneuvering could lead to
an epic romantic showdown outside the courtroom!*

*Read on for a sneak preview of
MAVERICK VS. MAVERICK
by Shirley Jump, the next book in the
MONTANA MAVERICKS: THE BABY BONANZA
continuity.*

"Dance with me."

Her eyes widened. "Dance…with you?"

"Come on." He swayed his hips and swung their arms. She stayed stiff, reluctant. He could hardly blame her. After all, just a few hours ago, they'd been facing off in court. "It's the weekend. Let's forget about court cases and arguments and just…"

"Have fun?" She arched a brow.

He shot her a grin. "I hear they do that, even in towns as small as Rust Creek Falls."

That made her laugh. Her hips were swaying along with his, though she didn't seem to be aware she was moving to the beat. "Are you saying my town is boring?"

Boring? She had no idea. But he wouldn't tell her that. Instead he gave her his patented killer smile. "I'm saying it's a small town. With some great music on the juke and a dance floor just waiting for you." He lifted her hand and spun her to the right, then back out again to the left.

"Come on, Ms. Dalton, dance with me. Me the man, not me the corporation you're suing."

She hesitated, and he could see his opportunity slipping away. Why did it matter that this woman—of all the women in this room, including the quartet flirting with him—dance with him?

"I shouldn't…" She started to slide her hand out of his.

He stepped closer to her. "Shouldn't have fun? Shouldn't dance with the enemy?"

"I shouldn't do anything with the enemy."

He grinned. "I'm not asking for anything. Just a dance."

Another song came on the juke, and the blonde and her friends started up again, moving from one side of the dance floor to the other. Their movements swept Walker and Lindsay into the middle of the dance floor, leaving her with two choices—dance with him or wade through the other women to escape.

For a second, he thought he'd won and she was going to dance with him. Then the smile on her face died, and she shook her head. "I'm sorry, Mr. Jones, but I don't dance with people who don't take responsibility for their mistakes."

Then she turned on her heel and left the dance floor and, a moment later, the bar.

Don't miss
MAVERICK VS. MAVERICK by Shirley Jump,
available October 2016 wherever
Harlequin® Special Edition books and ebooks are sold.

www.Harlequin.com

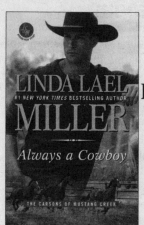

EXCLUSIVE
Limited Time Offer

$1.⁰⁰ OFF

New York Times bestselling author

LINDA LAEL MILLER

introduces you to the middle of the
three Carson brothers.

*He's as stubborn as they come—and he won't
thank a beautiful stranger for getting in his way!*

Always a Cowboy

Available August 30, 2016.
Pick up your copy today!

HQN™

$7.99 U.S./$9.99 CAN.

$1.⁰⁰ OFF   the purchase price of ALWAYS A COWBOY
by Linda Lael Miller.

Offer valid from August 30, 2016, to September 30, 2016.
Redeemable at participating retail outlets. Not redeemable at Barnes & Noble.
Limit one coupon per purchase. Valid in the U.S.A. and Canada only.

52614112

5 65373 00076 2   (8100)0 12202

A Romance FOR EVERY MOOD™

JUST CAN'T GET ENOUGH?

Join our social communities
and talk to us online.

You will have access to the latest
news on upcoming titles and special
promotions, but most importantly,
you can talk to other fans about your
favorite Harlequin reads.

Harlequin.com/Community

THE WORLD IS BETTER WITH

Romance

Harlequin has everything from contemporary, passionate and heartwarming to suspenseful and inspirational stories.

Whatever your mood, we have romance when you need it, wherever you are!

HARLEQUIN®

A *Romance* FOR EVERY MOOD™

www.Harlequin.com

#RomanceWhenYouNeedIt

Reading Has Its Rewards
Earn **FREE BOOKS!**

Register at **Harlequin My Rewards** and submit your Harlequin purchases from wherever you shop to earn points for free books and other exclusive rewards.

Join for FREE today at **www.HarlequinMyRewards.com**.